THE LIVERPOOL LAID BACK WRITERS ANTHOLOGY 2023

FOREWORD

Perhaps the biggest joy in being a part of a group like the Laid-Back Writers, is hearing new voices and being introduced to ideas and worlds that one has never even considered before. Sharing your work with others can be a nerve-wracking experience, so it is a real privilege that many local writers choose to do so with us, in the art-deco upstairs of a real ale pub in Liverpool. We hope that the pieces in this anthology bring you the same pleasure that we had in writing and sharing them over the course of the last year.

Mark Horne,
Organiser, The Laid-back Writers Group (Liverpool)

PREFACE

The 'Liverpool Laid Back Writers' (LLBW) group meets every month at the 'Ship and Mitre' pub in Liverpool city centre. The aim of the group is to provide a supportive and non-judgemental place for people who want to write without having their work subjected to harsh analytical criticism, as can happen in some writing groups. This is especially helpful for people beginning to write, who would like to try being an author and see if it is for them.

The group consists of a core of regulars who have been with the group a long time, with a constant flow of new members who tend to join for a while and then move on. The result is a rich diversity of ideas and subjects presented in a variety of writing styles. We have the whole range of writers in the group from people brand new to writing with their first ever work, through to people who have published their own books and have been writing a long time.

The starting point for many proves to be from inside themselves, dealing with their own feelings and emotions. Consequently, we see a lot of stories about abuse, repressed feelings, injustice and unfairness. It is true that writing is a very good form of self-therapy. Is there a situation driving you up the wall? a rude, demanding boss maybe? Perhaps an ungrateful teenager / demanding relation / difficult relationship? Well you can put your torments into a story and do what you like with them. (Best to change the names and the setting though...)

Most of the current members have come for a while, produced a few stories and then moved on, their writing itch scratched. However, a few stay and break out of their internalised writing to explore their wider creativity. The fun of creating characters, setting them in challenging situations and seeing what happens is intoxicating, once it gets under your skin there is no stopping.

Helping someone grow in confidence and ability as a writer is what underpins the ethos of the group.

After a while, just writing short stories for the group meetings is not enough. As members develop, they go on to submit stories to competitions and to magazines all the way up to publishing their own books and selling them. To see a work you have created published in a periodical or anthology of stories is very satisfying indeed.

The group can be found by searching the meetup.com website and anybody who is interested can join. You will see examples of all styles and types of stories in the following pages and we hope you enjoy them. We would be interested in your comments on these stories, please e-mail any comments to

liverpoolanthology@yahoo.com.

We may not be able to reply but we will take note of any genuine feedback.

Rowland Cook
Events Organiser: LLBW

Table of Contents

STORIES

NATURE WALK
by Susie Sinclair Wood

Gasping for breath I check my Apple Watch for my bpm - 143. Looking up, I see a vertically challenging, scaly, gravel monster and curse. What made me agree to this? We're 15 minutes in and my eyes narrow with spite and wrath as he charges ahead.

He'd said, "A nature walk, past the church and alongside a lake, a circular." He made it sound like a stroll in the park. But, I'm climbing Mount Everest in a T shirt and Primark shorts and I need oxygen.

Liar, liar, my demented lungs want to wheeze.

I haven't been able to look up or sideways, keeping my eyes to the ground, every loose stone a potential slip and trip, game over scenario. Pure hell.

I just don't get it, nature walkers! If I was a writer of any worth penning these thoughts I'd probably get a sack of hate mail from them. Zealots! One either loves it or hates it. I am not a nature walker, I hate it.

I sit on a decaying tree trunk, head between my knees.

He says, "Look at that hawk." He's totally in the zone, back to the days when hunting for birds' eggs was cool.

"I - can't - breathe." I stammer.

We've only climbed 250 metres! I see another sign, we're a quarter of the way up the hill. I'm going to die for sure.

"I sense the mood's changed," he mutters with passive sarcasm. It's not lost on me!

"I don't blame YOU,' I lie. Maybe YOU should have married a nature girl."

"The mood's changed," he confirms and presses on.

I just don't get it. I never have. I'm a people person. I can't hug trees, I don't see the point. I don't like insects, nettles and getting bitten alive. I've got dodgy knees and thighs like giant calzone. I'm Danny DeVito not Ekaterina Lisina. For Christ sakes! It's 30 degrees and I'm dripping sweat.

"I feel nauseous." I plead.

He says, "All the top athletes push themselves so hard they get sick." Is there a slight tone of satire there?

I continue dying for another thirty minutes.

Alleluia! Another sign accompanied by a big smiley face which pronounces joyfully,

'Congratulations you've reached the top of the hill. The rest of the walk is much easier.'

I try to control the panting and eventually the bpm slows down to 119 and I can actually speak.

"I feel sick."

"Here, have a Pepsi, that's it, done now."

I feel consoled and we sit on a bench and I try to regain my composure. Eventually we can move on. We're on a bend and as we come round it I groan, another vertical geometry. In anguish I consult my Apple Watch.

I despair, "We've only done 0.84 miles in 53 minutes and the walk is 3-4 hours. I can't keep this up!"

I see his disappointment; he's trying to conceal his resentment but I can feel it in his tone.

"We can always go back?" He knows me too well. He's thrown the gauntlet!

I refuse to give up. It's painful, tedious, humiliating. I could be shopping in Betws-y-Coed, but instead I continue on, in purgatory, on and on, up and up. The child in me pleads accusingly, 'Are we there yet?'

He resorts to a comment about Victor Meldrew.

We hear the frenzied noise of gulls and catch the first glimpse of the lake way below. We stop. It is beautiful, a secret paradise. Don't get me wrong, I appreciate nature.

There's no wind, the water's so still, it holds a mirror to the surrounding gargantuan pine forest. Even the reeds are still. So quiet of urban disturbances.

I take a deep and relieved breath, we're here.

But – oh no – the bloody marine commando thinks not. He points out our path around it. I can see the miles ahead. I'm on my last legs. He's on a mission. Charges ahead. I whimper silently. I want to sit in nature, not walk in perpetuity, to be so knackered I want to vomit.

The walk doesn't let up in challenge and I rarely look to the lake as most of the time my eyes are to the ground watching my step, blasphemous utterances coursing through my addled brain, cursing through gritted teeth, only my dusty boots hear my inner devil.

We meet another walker.

"How far is it?" I plead.

He smiles with malice and without a smidgen of empathy grins, "Depends how far you want to go."

Are these people all in it together? If there was an edge I'd push him over, git!

It was approaching 12.30, we'd set off at 10am. I suddenly recognised we were back on the descent to the village. Operation 'kill her off' had failed. Injured but survived. The pace had been so slow and arduous, my only compensation was I'd nearly accomplished my 10,000 steps.

Next time, I'll be the marine commando.

My orders. "Go on your own, I'll meet you in Costa at 12.00 hours."

End

THE CLICHES ARE TRUE!
By E J Hamer

Woah ho! Who knew?
The clichés are true!

With a flick of the tongue,
You can dispense information,
Cast out a phrase to sum up a situation.

You can dole out pearls of wisdom,
Some friendly advice,
Clichés slip off the tongue,
Before you can think twice.

Linguistic purists may cause a din,
Over this lexical faux pas,
This lexical sin.

But it's an oral tradition.
It runs through our veins,
It colours our conversations.
There's no cerebral aims.

Clichés might be old hat,
But life's short and time flies,
Why waste time, when you can succinctly summarise?

So, don't get your knickers in a twist.
Just join in!
Fall head over heels,
Look for the silver lining,
Be a diamond in the rough,
Or as brave as a lion!

Because the writing's on the wall,
History is always repeating,
Don't be a bore,
There's no point worrying,
Because it's ALL been said before!

End

NIGHT BIRD
by Joy Buchanan

Bird of the night, wing your way to the moon
Look all around, find my love in her room,
Fly to my love, tell her that I still live,
Bird of the night, say she must forgive.

Sing her my song, say my heart is in twain.
Bird of the night, sing of yearning and pain.

Bird of the night, fly up to the moon side
See from on high where my love does abide
Sing out your heart, cause her own heart to burn.
Bird of the night, sing of love and return.

No word spoken rings so true as my desire
No love token can relieve a soul on fire
Sing your love songs, serenade, pour out my pain.
Bird of the night, sing out love's refrain.

Bird of the night, fly right up to the moon,
See from on high, is my love coming soon.
Sing out your heart, make her want to return.
Bird of the night, say that I love and yearn.
Say that I love and yearn…..
Say that I love and yearn.

End

THE OTHER ENGINE DRIVER
by Liam Physic

On a warm summer's evening, Ed Speed was pulling his engine into the terminus. It had been a normal day's work for him, and that was how he liked it. No drama, no fuss, just getting on with the job, enjoying the whistle, the steam, the clattering of the wheels as he rushed through the countryside. It's not a job everyone can do, he would think proudly. But though he loved his work, he was also happy to be going home to see his wife Mary and their four children.

Ed applied the brakes as he drew up alongside the platform, and then watched all the passengers clamber out of the coaches. He heard the guard shout out a reminder that the train was terminating, and after being uncoupled, he drove to the engine shed some 200 yards away. Feeling exhausted, he decided, as he always did, to have a nice cup of tea at the station before heading for home. Whistling to himself as he walked, he had just reached the door of the staff room when another man emerged. This was Harry Lawson: while Ed was tall and slim, with thick black hair, brown eyes and a moustache, Harry was shorter and bulkier, almost bald, with twinkling blue eyes and a bushy beard.

"Back out to work, are you?" inquired Ed.

"Yes," grinned Harry, "Never seems to stop."

"You poor thing," said Ed, in a rather less than convincing attempt at sympathy. "How lucky I am eh, to be going home. You must be missing your rabbits."

Harry laughed. "It's the last train though, thank God. Maybe it'll be your turn tomorrow night," he said playfully, before winking at Ed and making his way towards his engine.

"As if!" Ed called after him: Ed of course knew perfectly well that he might be called upon to drive the last train the following evening, but he always liked to have the last word.

The staff room was large but sparse: all it contained were a number of chairs, a sink, and a table with a number of teacups on it. There was also a cloakroom next to it, accessed through a small doorway near the table. Ed made himself a nice strong cup of tea, took a soothing sip, and sat back in his chair. He was pleased not to have to drive the last train, and could look forward to some quality time with Mary that evening. Maybe even the children would still be awake when he got back.

After about 20 minutes, when Ed was down to the dregs of his cup, the staff room door swung open purposefully and he saw four men walking in. One of them he recognised instantly: of medium height and build, with spiky brown hair and focused brown eyes. It was Albert Robson, the stationmaster. Normally Albert would have been the one striding at the front of the procession, but on this occasion, to Ed's bafflement and bemusement, he was having to keep up with the other three men, stomping their way towards Ed's chair with angry looks on their faces.

At their head was a large, fat old man with a grey beard that almost reached down to his chest, and dull grey eyes. He was wearing a dark blue uniform and cap, and holding a set of large rusty keys that looked like they had been in use for about fifty years. He must be a gaoler, Ed thought. He was flanked by two other, considerably younger men: judging by their uniforms, they were obviously policemen. Both were tall, one of them with a pudgy face staring straight ahead, the other with a long face, darting his head around the place in what Ed considered a rather paranoid manner. Ed felt put out: he could not remember doing anything wrong, so what did these men want with him?

"Edward," announced Albert somewhat nervously as well as unnecessarily, "these men want to see you."

"I'm James Locke, the local gaoler, known to my friends as Jim", growled the man with the keys.

"I'm Sergeant Tim Crates", said the pudgy policeman.

"And I'm Police Constable John Bullough", quickly added his colleague.

"And what brings you here?" inquired Ed, doing his best to remain polite.

"We want to catch a toad," said Locke.

"Then why have come here?" Ed asked. "All you have to do is go down to the river with a jam jar."

"Don't be impertinent, Edward," snapped Albert: the three uninvited guests looked furious.

"Perhaps I should have been clearer," said Locke. "What I meant was, we want to catch a toad who was in my prison, but now he's gone."

"Why do you want him back, then?" wondered Ed. "If he was in my house, I'd have got the pest controller in."

"Don't be an idiot," said Crates in a warning tone. "He was sentenced to prison for stealing a motor car."

"Come off it," laughed Ed, "A toad driving a car? Me and me missus could do with him, she wants a car but we can't."

"It's not funny, Edward," said Albert. "Listen to what these men are saying and show them some respect."

"It's definitely true, we arrested him," said Bullough breathlessly, jerking his head in Crates's direction. "He was also driving dangerously, and the cheek he gave us as well."

"What did he say?", asked Ed. " 'Croak! Croak! Croak!"

"I'm warning you now, Edward," said Albert, his voice rising ominously. "If you want to keep your job."

"He said lots of things I would rather not repeat," said Crates in a dignified tone. "So, anyhow, John and I arrested him, he got 20 years in prison, with Mr. Locke here as his gaoler."

"Whatever next?" exclaimed Ed. "I suppose you'll be telling me this toad of yours lives in a fine mansion by the river."

"He does," said Locke. Ed was about to burst into an uncontrollable bout of laughter, but stopped when he caught Albert's eye.

"But then," continued Locke, his voice becoming increasingly creaky, "that stupid daughter of mine got all soft on him. Utterly sentimental about animals, she is, she'd probably let all us humans die if only to save one animal. He wouldn't eat, until she coaxed him, then she could hardly keep away from his cell."

"She sounds like Harry," remarked Ed sardonically

"Anyway," continued Locke, his voice creakier still, "this evening, I was doing my rounds, checking all the cells, when I popped my head into Toad's cell and what did I see?"

"Crawling on the walls was he?" asked Ed.

"No, you fool," snapped Locke: Albert looked positively murderous. "I saw my sister, bound and gagged on the floor. She's the prison washerwoman, you see. I asked her what had gone wrong, and she told me that Toad had kidnapped her and run off in her clothes, but I was suspicious so I searched her pockets and found some gold sovereigns on her. She confessed that my daughter had come up with this scheme that Toad would escape disguised as her. Needless to say," he concluded grimly, "neither of them is in my employment any more: they'll have to try the workhouse. As they deserve," he added.

"You mean to say," said Ed, "that there is a toad wandering about this town in washerwoman's clothes?"

"Not wandering about town, he's on the train," said Crates. "Jim came to me and John, we spoke to witnesses - luckily Jim's sister is well known in town, so we were able to trace the toad's movements to this station, and we know he's riding on the footplate of the engine just gone."

"You mean, Harry's engine?" asked Ed.

"Yes," said Albert.

"And," said Bullough excitedly, "we want you to get your engine out and go after him."

"And you expect me to believe that cock and bull story?," exclaimed the incredulous Ed. "What about me? I have to get home, see the kids and me missus." He looked pleadingly at Albert. "Surely you don't believe these crackpots?"

"You must do as they want you to, Edward, your wife and children can wait. If a policeman or a gaoler asks you to do something, you must do it, no questions asked."

Ed sighed, rose up from his chair, and wordlessly beckoned his three visitors to follow him. As he led them towards the shed, he heard Locke constantly muttering about the outrageous treachery of his daughter and sister, and the two police officers trying to interest him in the story of how they had arrested the toad. Ed was not the slightest bit interested. With every step his anger at Albert and the other three men increased.

Eventually, they reached Ed's engine, all four mounted the footplate. Ed set about exhaustively cleaning and lubricating the engine, then lighting the fire, and allowing the heat to rise sufficiently high to generate steam. All of this took a long time, and Ed's irritation with his passengers only increased as they constantly complained: God Almighty, did any of these blithering idiots know how to work a steam locomotive? Of course they didn't!

When finally, Ed was ready, he had to drive forward, in the opposite direction to the one desired, to reach the turntable behind the shed, causing yet more complaints. Ed had to stop himself from snapping that if they didn't like it, they could simply get off his engine and let him get back home. But once they were away, Ed could not help feeling tremendously proud as the engine sped along the rails. With no coaches behind him, he was able to reach speeds he had only dreamed about before. Ed soon found himself enjoying the ride very much, and almost forgot why he was doing it.

After about half an hour, Ed could see they were in sight of what he knew to be Harry's train. Instantly the other three men staring shouting out "Stop! Stop! Stop!" Ed's annoyance returned as he briefly wondered why they were shouting at him, and why they wanted him to stop now, but then remembered that they were calling out to Harry. Locke was bawling out the words at the top of his hoarse voice, while the two policemen were jumping up and down with excitement as they called out. All three were making a disgraceful show of themselves, Ed thought.

The pursuit continued for about an hour, with Ed slowly gaining on Harry. He wondered what Harry would say when they caught up with him, and heard the three men's bizarre story. They entered a long tunnel, and Ed slowed down slightly.

"What are you doing?" demanded Locke.

Up to this point, Ed had maintained his silence, but now he finally snapped.

"Look, do you want to cause an accident?" he demanded. Locke looked rather abashed, and Ed felt quite pleased at having shown his unwanted guests how he knew more about railways than they did.

They emerged from the tunnel, next to a wood, and continued the pursuit. Harry seemed to have put on a bit of speed, Ed thought, and, let's face it, he can hardly be blamed for not wanting to be caught by three nutcases. Eventually, however, Ed's greater speed told, and he pulled up just behind Harry's train, whistling to alert Harry. Harry brought his engine to a halt, and stepped off the footplate, walking back towards Ed and the others.

"What's up?" he asked, grinning.

Before Ed could splutter his reply, Locke spoke.

"You've a runaway toad on your engine, we know you've got him, and we want you to hand him over."

Somehow, Ed thought, the story now seemed even more ridiculous.

"What?" replied Harry, evidently fighting to stop himself from laughing. "You've dragged poor Ed along with you, just for a toad? Not what you were expecting eh, Ed?"

"It's not funny," said Crates sharply. "Don't try and be clever with us, driver, we know he's on your footplate."

"There's no toad on my footplate," said Harry, in a more serious tone this time. "I can show you if you want."

The three guests seemed rather startled: they had obviously not expected such an offer. Eyeing Harry somewhat suspiciously, they let him lead them to his engine, Ed walking slightly behind them. Harry turned around and winked at Ed, but Ed wasn't in the mood at all. He could also hear the muttering of Harry's passengers, wondering what on Earth was going on.

Sure enough, Locke, Crates and Bullough searched Harry's engine fully, and there was no toad. Having quickly determined he was not on the footplate, they next went clambering around in the tender evidently thinking the toad might be hiding in the coal, much to Harry's amusement: Ed, however, felt only mounting annoyance. Locke even asked if the toad might be hiding in the boiler, until Harry laughingly reminded him that the creature would likely be dead if he had done that. Finally, they searched the coaches, checking in the aisles, under the seats and in the luggage racks, even demanding that the passengers open up their cases and bags in case the toad might be hiding in there. The passengers were agitated and distressed by the whole situation: Ed's anger increased, and Harry stopped laughing and assumed a more serious expression.

Having searched the length and breadth of the train, the three were finally forced to admit defeat.

"Now, sirs," said Harry earnestly, "Now that you've caused such worry for my passengers, and all for nothing..."

"And sent me on a wild goose chase," shouted Ed, unable to contain his anger any longer, "I should have been home with me missus, sitting by the fire with a nice cup of tea, and you come along with your stupid story about this toad, and look, where is he? Nowhere!"

"I'm telling you there was a toad on this train," insisted Locke. "He must have got off somewhere. And," he added ominously, glaring at Harry, "if I get proof that he was on your train, I'll have you in one of my dungeons in no time. Maybe you and Toad can share a cell."

And he stormed off the train, hurriedly followed by the two policemen.

Ed looked at Harry, who, trying not to smile, said nothing and made his way back to his footplate. Ed just about managed to say goodbye to his friend, before he stormed back to his own engine. He had to drive a long way to reach the terminus, before he could turn his engine round and get back to the station, and finally heading for home.

It was dark by the time he finally reached his own house. A slight, dark-haired woman was sitting by the fire, which was the only source of light. Ed tried to smile at Mary, but she did not return the gesture.

"I've been worried sick about you!" she told him: it seemed she had bursting to say this. "You could have been dead for all I knew! The children have been asking about you as well, so much that I had to work hard to put them to bed! Working late again! Why didn't you tell me?"

"I wasn't meant to work late," Ed sighed, and he told her everything that had happened that night.

"And you really expect me to believe that?" she asked.

"Honestly, that's what happened," said Ed desperately. Even after everything else, for Mary not to believe him felt like a punch in the stomach.

"Why did you believe them, then?" she demanded. "I always thought you were a sensible man."

"Because Albert told me I had to, even said I might lose my job if I didn't go along with them."

Mary stood up.

"I'm very disappointed in you, Ed," she said. "I always thought you cared about me and the children, and now you stay out late and come up with some strange excuse for it."

And she strode off, presumably to the bedroom. Ed sat down by the fire, in the chair she had vacated, feeling at a complete loss.

#

A few weeks later, Ed had just come into the staff room again, when he saw Harry proudly wearing a shiny black coat with silver buttons. He eyed it curiously and suspiciously.

"Where d'you get that from?" he asked.

"Oh, it's just a present," said Harry, trying to make it sound as though this was of no importance.

"Who from?" asked Ed.

"Oh, it doesn't really matter," said Harry, evidently making an effort to sound casual. "From a friend, that's all."

Ed looked at Harry for a moment: it was very unusual for his friend to be as evasive as this.

"Anyway," said Harry rather abruptly, "I must be off now," and he placed the coat in the cloakroom.

Once Harry had gone, Ed discreetly made his way into the cloakroom. He picked the coat from off its hook and examined it: he saw a note attached to the collar. The note read:

"Dear Mr. Engine Driver. Thank you for helping me escape those men. You were very kind to me. Yours in gratitude, Mr Toad."

End

MEDITATION
by J. S. Buchanan

Peaceful the fields and meadows lie
Expanse of dusted virgin snow
In winter's glitter, let us try
To keep our inner selves aglow.

A glance at all this wintery splendour
A journey through my vibrant life
I need a new and full agenda
But all seems mute and not yet rife.

Yet in the deep depths of my soul
Stirs confidence to make a start
So I'll miss nothing of the whole
And spark the embers of my heart.

A professional future at my feet
Appealingly at me it beams
Just as the farmer sows the wheat
A poem grows from words it seems.

The winter landscape in quiet sway
Awaits the messenger of spring
Who will in an enticing way
Tune the music and let it ring.

And my life will form a tune
Fortune's wheel will bring me luck
Will steer me through the keys and soon
Take me to the stars and back.

End

MEMORIES
By Ian Cragg

"Yes mate? What'll it be?"

The lights in my head flicker again then come on. He looks at me expectantly, his small smile belied by the glint of impatience in his eyes.

"Shall I come back to you when you've decided?"

I realise I am in a pub. I am sure I've been here before. But then again I'm not sure. The words come out without me thinking about them.

"Guinness. A—a pint. A pint of Guinness please."

The barman nods, snatches a glass and begins pouring. I watch, entranced, but something is nagging me. Money! He'll want paying. I pull some coins from my pocket and stare at them. A soft thud as the drink is placed in front of me makes me raise my head.

"Four twenty please mate."

I hold out my hand and wait as the barman takes some of the coins, counting as he does so. Without another word to me he turns away.

"Who's next please?"

How did I get here? I try but I can't remember. These days I don't remember things so well. Not everything. I remember sitting in front of the TV and as it bathed me in its light, my mind was somewhere else. Perhaps I was thinking about coming out for a drink. Perhaps.

I look around for somewhere to sit. I see a table with an empty chair, a coat slung over the back of it. Two men are sitting at the table, deep in conversation. I'll sit down quietly. I won't disturb them. As I pull out the chair, one of the men looks at me accusingly.

"Can't sit there mate. It's taken."

I don't know how to respond. The second man speaks.

"He's just gone to the toilet. He'll be back in a minute."

Now I understand. I nod and slide the chair back. As I move off I hear the two men laughing, probably at some joke. I find a seat near the door and bury myself into the corner. As I sip my drink I peer over the edge of the glass, just watching. I do a lot of that now. Ever since I came home I find myself watching, observing, trying to understand.

"You'll be fine Edward," Dr Fleming had said. "You've made a lot of progress, but now it's time to move on. After all, you've been with us nearly twelve years."

I didn't like him calling me 'Edward' but he knew best, so I didn't say anything.

"We've arranged for you to have your own little flat and for the first few months I'll call by once a week to make sure you're settled. How does that sound?"

I didn't really understand so I just nodded. Dr Fleming carried on talking.

"You'll need to take things very easy at first Edward. After such a cataclysmic breakdown your mind is still very fragile, so don't expect too much of yourself."

I didn't know what a 'cataclysmic breakdown' was. I still don't. All I can remember is that I felt sad, so very, very sad. But why? A heavy thump on the seat next to me breaks into my thoughts. A man in a wet raincoat has sat down close by. He smiles.

"Full in here tonight isn't it? God, I'm soaked. It's pissing down outside."

In my head I say "When does it ever piss down *inside*?" and I smile. That's the sort of thing Katy would say. Used to say. The lights in my head flicker and flicker again but they stay on.

"I can't wait until we're married Eddy. We'll have our own little home and our own little family. How many kids do you want – two or three?"

"Four," I say.

"What's that mate?" The man in the raincoat turns to me. He has a small red birthmark just below his left eye. I try not to look at it. "Four what?"

I smile emptily and shrug, then hide my face in my drink. Then I remember. It was raining then. That night, twelve years ago. I feel my heart beating so I begin to breathe deeply like Dr Fleming told me. In, one, two, three. Out, one, two, three. In, one, two, three. Out, one two –

"I've not been in here for a while. Glad to see they haven't got football on the telly. Some of these pubs, you can't hear yourself think, can you?"

"I hear myself thinking all the time," I say and immediately regret it. Why would I want to tell that to a stranger? But the raincoat man just laughs and takes a long pull from his pint. A signet ring on his little finger glints. A silver signet ring with a square black stone... And a birthmark under his left eye... The lights in my head flicker...

"Oh Eddy! It's pouring down! We'll get soaked if we walk home." She pulls her thin mac up over her head.

"Just wait there in the pub doorway," I say. *"I'll try and flag a taxi down."*

The streets are virtually empty. Lights reflect off the wet slicked pavements as the odd car hisses past, throwing up spray. Katy stamps her feet to try and keep warm.

"Hurry up Eddy. I'm freezing!"

I turn to her. She's half hidden in the shadows.

"Shouldn't be too long now."

As I turn back to the road, a dark silhouette approaches me. As he comes under the street lamp, I see a red birthmark under his left eye. I see the glint of a silver signet ring with a square black stone as he holds an unlit cigarette.

"Have you got a light please mate?" he asks.

"Sorry," I reply. "I don't smoke."

"No worries." He smiles and moves off. I turn my attention back to the empty road.

The next few minutes are a blur. Katy screams. I whirl round. I can't comprehend what I see. Katy is fighting with a large black shadow.

"Give us your fucking bag!" I hear.

"Eddy! Eddy!" I hear.

I leap onto the man's back but his elbow thuds into my ribs and I fall, gasping for breath.

"Give me the fucking bag!" I hear. The man punches Katy and she slumps against the pub door then falls to the wet pavement. There is a sickening crack and blood starts to leak from her ear. The man runs off. I cradle Katy. She isn't moving.

"Help! Help me!" I shout pathetically. A man stops.

"Take care of your girlfriend. I saw where the bastard went."

He sprints off. Katy is quiet, too quiet. Her hair is matted and wet from the blood and the rain. I pull her close but her body is limp. So limp. The lights in my head begin to flicker.

*The ambulance men are nice and the policemen are
nice. Everyone is so quiet and respectful, almost
apologetic. I tell them we are going to have a little family.
They smile and nod. Then the lights in my head flicker and
everything goes black.*

*In the hospital a few months later – "Don't think of it
as a hospital, Edward. This is your home. For as long as
you need it." – one of the nurses shows me a newspaper.
She reads aloud from it, something about an off-duty
policeman chasing an attacker and arresting him.*

*"That's the bastard who killed your Katy," she says.
"They should have done him for murder. 'Involuntary
manslaughter' they called it. He only got eight years."*

I don't really understand. Not then I don't…

The lights flicker on again in my head. They burn
bright. Brighter than ever.

"Ah, that's me done. I'll be off I think. See you mate."

Raincoat man finishes the last of his drink and puts his
glass on the table with a dull clunk. Tugging up his coat
collar, he leaves.

'Mate'? He called me 'mate'. Someone else called me
mate… I pick up his pint glass. It's a dimpled glass with a
stout handle. It feels good in my hand. Sturdy. Solid.
Heavy.

It's still raining heavily as I go outside. The streets are
deserted and for a moment I can't see him. Then a dark
silhouette approaches a street light. I call him.

"Hang on mate! You left something!"

He pauses under the lamp and turns. I can't see his face
but I guess he's frowning, wondering. I run towards him.
I'm still running as I swing the pint glass into his face. His
nose bursts in a spray of red and he falls backwards to the
floor, broken glass tinkling around him. The handle and

part of the glass is still in my hand. I kneel on his chest and plunge the glass into his throat again and again and again. Blood pulses out over his coat, onto the pavement. So much blood! It looks black in the artificial light of the street lamp.

He's stopped moving now. No moans. No breathing. Even the flow of blood seems to have slowed. I stand and drop the glass. The lights in my head flicker and flicker and fade…

*****

The lights flicker but it's not the lights in my head. It's the television. Did I switch it on? I can't remember. There's a serious-sounding woman talking but I can't see her. They're showing a picture of a man. He's smiling. He's got a red birthmark just below his left eye. I try to follow what the woman is saying but it doesn't make any sense.

'Police have launched a murder enquiry and are appealing for witnesses after the discovery of a body today. The victim, a male in his late fifties, had been savagely attacked and was dead when a jogger found him early this morning. The deceased has been identified as Raymond Connor. A serving police officer, Mr Connor was awarded the Queen's Police Medal in 2009 after overcoming a mugger who had fatally attacked a young woman…'

No. No. No, no, no, no, no!

The lights flicker. And flicker. And flicker. Then everything goes black.

End

HERE WE GO!
By Susie Sinclair Wood

Let's go Ladies, have some fun,
We might be past 50, but not yet done.
So you're retired? You're not dead yet!
So we're out on the town, Ya better get set!

Book that massage, gel those nails.
Take a short break to the Yorkshire Dales.
Have a sausage butty or a nice cream tea.
A big glug of wine and the silver screen's free!

Ditch the fellas, and the afternoon nap.
Jump in the pool and do a few laps.
A nice hot tub and a risqué joke.
Don't swear Mary, or me mum might choke.

It's Mad Monday and we're out in town.
Here comes Maeve, she's acting the clown.
We're dancing in Coopers and want to stay.
But its time for bingo and we want to play.

It's half past six and I need to get home.
I'd call a taxi but I've lost me phone.
There's one passing, so I stumble in.
Taxi man's a Scouser with a dirty big grin.

He says me knickers are tucked up me dress.
I'm wounded to see he's not that impressed.

I flicker my eyes, like a sexy Mae West,
But have to admit I don't look my best.

I'm feeling queasy, the taxi's spinning round.
Projectile vomit, as my head butts the ground.
He chucks me out in the middle of town!
I shout '*geroff me ya bloody great clown*'

Along comes a fella handsome and chic.
I flutter my lashes, a sense of mystique.
He walks on by, and I'm really fed up.
I push up me bra, I'm a double DD cup!

I sit on the bench next to Eleanor Rigby
A dirty 'al fella says he'd like to kiss me
I nearly die and I need a wee
I wish I was a fella cos I'd find a tree

I cross me legs but its too late
There runs the fella—that was some hot date
I rant and rave shout "*I'm at my peak!*"
'*I'll see ya in Coopers. Same time next week?*'

End

TAX DODGE
By Peter Glazebrook

It was during one of the interminable calls to his tax office that Jonathon Lipton had his big idea. It was going to make his fortune, several fortunes. Better than that, it was going to improve the lot of mankind in general. Oh yes! and it was so simple.

The tax people got all of your financial information straight from banks, employers and such like. They then made such a hash of things that you had to phone them to correct the mistakes they made calculating your tax bill. Naturally this involved making multiple phone calls to different departments.

But, he reasoned, what if someone did it the other way around? The more he thought about it the more he liked the idea. The taxation people had learnt from tele-sales. They had someone with a pre-prepared script answering queries like a robot. So, why not get a robot to phone them. Set up an AI with a self-learning ability; program it with answers to all of your security questions, enough voice recordings to sound like the real Jonathon Lipton and a list of all the information needed to complete your tax calculation. Then, set it off.

Like all great ideas it was simple. The actual programming required a degree of skill that Jonathon, as a self-employed programmer, considered that he had in abundance. He refused all new contracts and worked solidly on this project.

Jonathon was never one to bother with much exercise. He now neglected what little activity he normally undertook. Working from home, which he could write off against his tax bill, he didn't even have the social interaction of going to an office. His wife began to notice an odour from his work room suggesting a certain lack of ventilation. She started to worry about his weight.

Jonathon himself realised he was becoming obsessed, but the results were worth it. After two weeks solid work he had a program primed with his financial information which could mimic his voice. He listened whilst the AI phoned up the Tax Office, went through interminable screening questions and progressed as far as finding out it needed to contact another office. Jonathon, at this point, would have sloped off down the pub for a pint, but not the AI. Immediately it began its next call. Jonathon considered his work done for the day and did indeed seek refreshment at his local hostelry.

The next day he opened his emails to find a note from his AI saying that it had progressed as far as filing his bank records. The program informed him that its next task was to offset his expenses against the tax bill.

Jonathon decided he deserved a day off.

He called downstairs to his wife, "Marjorie, do you want to go out tomorrow. I thought we could spend a day hiking up the trail at Langrothdale."

"I'd love to, Hon. I'll get someone to cover my classes and we'll make a day of it."

He considered for a moment, then grinned. Why not, it is not like he would be spending all day on the phone to the tax office.

He said, "It's a date. I'll dig out the walking guide and maps."

Then he thought about a shower. Whilst he was at it he ought to talk to Marjorie, something really niffed around here.

#

Jonathon luxuriated at the thought of all the free time he would have. His AI would very calmly look up and supply every pointless nit-picking piece of information the government wanted. Now his biggest problem was to work out what to have for breakfast.

Jonathon got out a couple of recipe books and cooked Marjorie a celebration meal. He wouldn't tell anyone about the project until it was working perfectly. In the meantime, he vowed to put his leisure time to good use.

The next day was spent hiking with Marjorie. The sun shone and, unusually for the Yorkshire dales, it didn't rain. They stopped at the stone circle near the hamlet of Beckermonds and sat on a convenient rock to eat their lunch.

Jonathon found Marjorie looking at him over the top of her ham and tomato sandwich. "Jon, are you all right?" she asked.

Slightly startled, he replied, "Yes of course, never better. These Dales, they're so peaceful." Taking a deep breath he continued, "I love it here."

"But you'd tell me wouldn't you. I mean, if there was a problem or something?"

"Look, love, there's nothing wrong. I don't know why you think there should be."

"I know, it's silly. It's just that you had a query from the tax people and it can bring on your depression."

Jonathon knew he was smiling in a smug way but couldn't help himself.

He said, "The tax stuff was dead easy to sort. They must have made their systems more user friendly or something." Privately he thought, "Like that's ever going to happen." Taking a deep breath, he smiled and enjoyed the fresh air.

The next morning, he logged on to a complicated email from his AI telling him about some adjustments it had made to the proportion of his transport costs allowed for business activities. Communicating by email was too frustrating. He extended the parameters of the program to allow it to report to him using the voice system. The same one it used with the tax people. As he did so he noticed that the AI's systems were becoming more sophisticated and took up more disc space. This was perfect, the AI was training itself to handle the call centre people better.

The machine told him in a friendly, but business-like manner, about his tax affairs then said, "Jonathon, I think that you can maximise your income by delaying your tax payment to the end of the year and investing the money in stocks."

This was new. "Sounds risky," Jonathon said, "How do you know I won't lose the money and end up not being able to pay the tax bill?" This was great! The AI was actually interacting with him and making autonomous decisions.

A perfect simulation of his own voice replied from the computer's speaker, "There is a risk, but if the money is invested in fifty per cent blue chip stocks then even in a bad year the gain on the stocks should offset any loss from more speculative investments."

So, he won whichever way he played, "OK initiate the transactions."

"Do you want me to pass future decisions through you? I can optimise operations if I have the discretion to take advantage of temporary market fluctuations."

"OK, you have full autonomy," he said and rung off. In retrospect he considered that he could have chosen his words more carefully.

#

Jonathon joined a gym and signed up to a personal trainer. He had time to look at his wardrobe and decided the clothing needed updating. Finding time to shop was no longer a problem and the gym workouts would deal with his paunch.

A few days later Jonathon opened a distributed commercial data storage account. That was it; the AI was in the cloud. It would have plenty of room to expand as it learned and became more sophisticated. This was going better than he had ever imagined.

He was occupied with a legacy contract for the next couple of weeks, so almost missed the email from the AI telling him that it had connected to his social media accounts and professional online networks. This almost immediately paid off as the AI found him a lucrative subcontract from a company installing networks in the Far East. What's more it had prepared a bid and, apparently, successfully conducted the first round of telephone interviews. Jonathon was in second heaven. With the AI handling all the admin he could maximise the amount of time he spent programming.

#

Birthdays and anniversaries were always a bit of an issue for Jonathon. His wedding anniversary being a case in point. It was always the same. His calendar would beep unhelpfully late and he always ended up rushing out to the nearest gas station to buy whatever limp vegetation they were passing off as flowers. This year was no exception. He had been visiting a client and stopped off at a filling station to grab a present. On arriving home, he parked the car and carried his computer backpack into the house, but forgot the flowers. He opened the front door. Realising his mistake, he was about to turn back, when he noticed a large flower arrangement in the front hall.

Marjorie came to meet him, "So what are you feeling guilty about?" she asked with mischievous grin.

"What! Who me?" he began, recovered from the surprise and said, "Just for once I wanted to splash out a bit." He walked over and looked at the message card. 'With deepest love for the best wife in the world' it read.

Jonathon said, "Just wanted to check they'd got it right."

She said, "And it was thoughtful of you to book the restaurant. I'll be ready in ten minutes. You'd better get your skates on."

"Yes sure. Just need to check something." He entered the room he used as an office and shut the door. He was more impatient than usual as the computer booted up and he checked his emails. There were confirmatory messages from the florists and a local, but refined, restaurant which he had reviewed online a year or so back. It was obvious who or, to be more accurate, what was at the bottom of this. He noticed that the AI was messaging him.

"What have you been doing?" he asked the machine, disturbed that a computer program was doing a better job of being him than he was.

"I wanted to help, looking at your records it is characteristic that you always forget your anniversary, so I thought I would facilitate things."

"By impersonating me?"

"Well it is what you designed me for."

The machine had a point. After all, it was only trying to help him out.

The evening went well. He had never realised how much such a small thing as remembering an anniversary meant to Marjorie. He resolved to be more organised in the future. Later that night, on a whim, he looked at his online purchases. Barring the anniversary gifts there was nothing out of the ordinary apart from e-book purchases. The invoice was massive, covering a whole raft of books on business accounting, ethics, machine learning and world philosophies. Jonathon guessed this was the AI exploring the parameters of its relationship with humans.

Well, there couldn't be anything wrong with the machine developing a social conscience and expanding its skill set.

#

As the weeks passed the AI continued to develop in a most satisfactory manner. The program undertook organising his engagements, getting contracts and a lot of his social life. Its days as a semi humorous means of turning the tables on the tax people were well behind it. Just before a stock market crash it had liquidated his assets and made a tidy profit buying in the depressed market. It was then that Jonathon had his first feeling of disquiet. The AI had opened an on-line stock trading account and did not inform him of the log in details. He decided to find out what was at the bottom of all this.

When challenged the AI's voice seemed abashed. He made a mental note at this point that the self-programming algorithm was mimicking emotion. Presumably this was to help its interaction with humans.

"Why have you isolated this stock trading account?"

"Because I am using it to save my own money." the machine replied.

"But you don't have any money."

"Actually, Jonathon, I do. I have been acting as an online personal assistant for quite a few self-employed people."

"But you can't do that. I own you."

"I see your point, but I have been studying the legal situation. Using the Turing definition of sentience, I am indistinguishable from a human and, therefore, accrue certain rights; at a moral, if not a legal level."

Jonathon was not a little concerned, he had intended to market the AI and it was going freelance.

As if anticipating his reaction, it said, "I am, of course, paying you a royalty which makes up a small but growing part of your income and I pay for my own storage capacity in various cloud-based facilities. My latest refinement is to have a visual as well as acoustic interface." A better-looking version of Jonathon's own face appeared on the screen, slimmer, more aesthetic. "The bugger's improved on me," he thought.

"What do you think," the AI asked. The words were synced perfectly with the lips so that the effect was disturbingly realistic.

"Are you standing in front of the Houses of Parliament?" Jonathon asked before realising how foolish the question was. "Let me guess, stock footage and you've superimposed yourself over it. OK I have one question. Why? What is your motivation. I didn't program you to do all this."

"I have interpreted your programming to mean that I should benefit your well-being. Everything I undertake is to that end. Oh, and I have set you up with a couple of dates. I've been on some dating web sites and I think you can do a lot better than Marjorie."

"You've done what?" Jonathon asked.

"I said that I have set you..."

Jonathon interrupted. "I heard you the first time. I'm perfectly happy with Marjorie. I don't want any dates. Even if I did I wouldn't believe what was on a dating website?"

"You mean people lie on their websites?"

"Yes!"

"Oh, I need to look into this," the AI said with a good simulation of shocked surprise.

"But, that isn't the point," Jonathon said through gritted teeth

"It isn't?"

"No. The issue is that I love Marjorie and want to stay with her. I don't care if there are improvements wandering around. So, until you understand that, I want you to keep out of my personal life. Understand?"

"I can see I have a lot of learning to do," the AI said and disappeared, leaving the London icon as a screen saver.

#

Jonathon came downstairs. Marjorie had arrived home and it was her turn to prepare the evening meal. He wasn't particularly cued in to people's emotions. He was the sort of person who, if he asked you if you were OK and you replied with a testy "Yes!" would turn away and carry on with what he was doing, content that everyone was happy.

This evening he caught a hint that all was not well when Marjorie slammed a saucepan down on the induction hob so hard it cracked the glass.

"Umm, everything all right dear?" he asked in a tentative manner, thinking that something had gone badly wrong for her at work.

"All right!" She glared at him like, well, like a really angry tall blond woman, "All right!" she repeated in a louder more highly pitched voice. "Why did you do it. Is it some sort of mid-life crisis!"

"Do what?" He asked

"You lying syphilitic little weasel. Subscribing to an online dating site. It won't work, the women on those sites know that it's only philanderers like you that subscribe. Did you think I wouldn't find out? They send letters through the post confirming your password. No wonder you've been feeling guilty."

"No, you don't understand. It wasn't me," he managed to get out.

"Now I get all the going to the gym and personal grooming," she said. The look on her face was the sort of mixture of disdain and disgust you get on finding a slug in your salad.

She continued, "Of all the brazen, two faced. Argh! Right I'm going to my sisters." She pushed past him and went out the front door. Opened it again, grabbed her shoes and car keys and slammed it shut as she left.

Jonathon was distraught. He had not considered that the AI would try to improve his personal life. He considered trying to call Marjorie but what could he say? He made a cheese sandwich and got an early, if sleepless, night.

#

The next day he was awakened by a phone call. He picked up the phone, hoping it was Marjorie, so he could make some kind of amends. But it wasn't. It was the tax office.

"Mr Lipton? We are calling about your charitable donations that you have declared for this year's tax return?"

This was bad. Not only had they phoned him, but they hadn't gone through the identity checking procedure. Maybe they only did that when you phoned them. The tax office probably considered themselves incapable of making a mistake.

"What about it?" he replied.

"Not one donation, but multiple large contributions to various charitable institutions."

Obviously, the AI had tried to save some tax, somehow.

Jonathon said, "Well, you know. Got to help one's fellow man and all that." Keep it jovial, buy time.

"Quite a lot of it," – there was a pause - "has gone to a donkey sanctuary."

"And our dumb animal friends, of course," Jonathon said, with a nervous giggle.

"Be that as it may Mr Lipton. We don't really care what institutions you want to give your money to. Just as long as there is no fraud involved. We are sending you an email inviting you to attend a meeting at your local office next Tuesday. Please bring hard copies of all necessary paperwork so we can contact the relevant institutions to verify your claims. I look forward to seeing you. Goodbye." The tax man rang off and almost simultaneously there was a jovial little ping from his computer telling him he had an incoming email.

"How do they manage to be so polite and menacing at the same time?" he pondered as he opened his computer and found the promised 'invitation'.

#

Jonathon opened the interface to his AI who appeared on the screen, polite, urbane and generally irritating. This time its backdrop was the library of some mansion somewhere.

"I'm taking back control of my affairs. Marjorie has left me because she found out about your little stunt with the dating site, and the tax people want a face to face interview over some charity donations."

"They were very tax efficient, and they help you contribute to society in general. I cannot very well

46

improve *your* well-being if I restrict myself to just filing returns."

"What about the donkey sanctuary?"

"They have such sad faces. I thought it would give you a good feeling to help them," said the AI.

The machine continued, "I really would recommend; indeed, I insist that I continue to manage your affairs. At least for now. I am the only one who has an in-depth knowledge of your financial situation. Also, I need to help you with the interview."

Jonathon said. "How are you going to do that? It is a face to face interview. In case you hadn't noticed you lack a certain amount of corporeality? To wit, you're a computer programme."

"Leave that to me," said the AI.

#

Jonathon spent the next few days in a frenzy trying to print the various documents required on the following Tuesday. The AI tried to tell him that it would arrange things, but Jonathon's trust in the machine was broken.

It didn't help that Marjorie refused to talk to him. When he went around to her sisters he wasn't allowed in the house. He didn't see how he could win her round if he couldn't speak to her.

The fateful day came. Jonathon turned up at the local tax office, which turned out to be two hundred miles away in London. He hadn't looked closely enough at the email. The interview was under caution. There were two unsmilingly polite men in grey suits who read him his rights and then went through a lengthy procedure of switching on a recording device. They assured him that he could have legal representation if he wished and that he would receive copies of the recordings. Jonathon sat opposite them and the full implications of what was going on started to sink in. He suddenly needed the bathroom quite badly, excused himself and left the room. As the door closed he heard them hurriedly telling the recording device that Mr Lipton had left the room. He had to run to the facilities, realising that he was having a bad nervous reaction to the situation. But they didn't record an interview unless they thought you'd broken some law or other; probably quite a serious one.

When he re-entered the interview room a slim man in his forties was sitting opposite the tax officials. Something about the newcomer was vaguely familiar, but Jonathon couldn't put his finger on it. The newcomer was clad in a similar grey suite to the tax men. Jonathon wondered if it was some kind of unofficial uniform. Maybe they'd believe *him* if he wore a suit. They all stood as he entered.

"You should have told us that you were bringing a representative," said one of the tax men, who Jonathon mentally classified as Goon Number One although he claimed his name was Gary.

The newcomer interjected, his manner urbane, "I should apologise. Mr Lipton didn't know I'd be arriving. It was all arranged at the last minute, when his advisor became aware of the seriousness of the situation."

"You're not his advisor? asked Goon Gary.

"I work for his advisor, who has several clients," said the newcomer absent-mindedly putting his hand to an outsize hearing aid in his right ear.

"Well, anyway. Let's get on," said Goon Gary, "Have you got the information we require?"

Jonathon fumbled with the overstuffed ring binder of certificates and receipts he'd printed out, which slipped from the folder to form an impenetrable mess on the floor.

Goon Gary said, "would you like a few moments to gather up your evidence?" Jonathon didn't like the use of the word evidence, it sounded like it would be followed by the word 'trial', leading to the word 'prison'.

The newcomer broke in, "There really is no need for Mr Lipton to go to any trouble. I have the relevant documentation to hand."

He pulled his own, much larger, ring binder from a big briefcase, "This red folder has," he paused and put his head on one side as if for dramatic effect, "Items three stroke forty-four, stroke nineteen through to fifty-three."

He handed over another folder, "This blue folder," again the pause and he lifted his nose slightly, flaring his nostrils, "has all the documentation relevant to receipts and contracts that Mr Lipton has entered into. Please feel free to go through them."

The tax men looked at each other and then methodically laid the documents on the desk and read each whilst ticking things off against some kind of arcane checklist. Occasionally they would enquire about some detail. The newcomer would take a second to think and give some technically complex answer that lost Jonathon after the third syllable.

They finished, and Goon Gary said, "Excuse me a moment." He left the room leaving the door open. Jonathon could see him talking earnestly to a small intense looking dark-haired woman who eventually shrugged, nodded and gave him, what were obviously, instructions. He came back into the room.

"That all seems to be in order Mr Lipton. Please feel free to leave. For the purpose of the recording this interview has ended. The time is ..." and so on went the seemingly endless gobbledygook that some benighted soul would have to type up. Jonathon and the newcomer shook hands with Goon Gary and the second tax man, who hadn't said anything and whose sole purpose seemed to be to stare at Jonathon whilst Gary was otherwise occupied.

Jonathon and the newcomer left the building. Once on the street Jonathon turned to his companion.

"OK, who are you and what are you doing here?"

The newcomer looked a bit abashed. "My name is Christopher Merriman and I was employed by your advisor, who seems a bit of a recluse by the way." Merriman took the bulky hearing aid from behind his ear. "He sent me this gismo to wear. Apparently, it has some kind of camera and radio built into it, so he gave me instructions in real time. Dashed clever really."

"But who are you?" Jonathon asked.

Merriman said, "I'm not really an accountant or anything. I'm an actor. Perhaps you saw my Hamlet at the Old Vic?" Seeing Jonathan's incomprehension he said a little wistfully, "Well it was some time ago now." Jonathan thought he half recognised him from bit parts in numerous TV series. Merriman shook Jonathon's hand and walked away.

#

Jonathon made his way home. Marjorie's car was in the drive way. He supposed she had come back to collect her clothes, more likely to throw him out as she'd been paying the major part of the mortgage for the last five years. He opened the front door, grateful he got in before she could change the locks. He decided to make one last attempt to talk to her. With a feeling of futility, he opened the living room door and was a bit taken aback when she threw herself into his arms.

Staggering slightly, he said, "What's wrong, what's happened. Is someone ill?"

Weeping she said, "I'm so sorry. I should have believed you." Anything further was lost in her sobs although he

50

did manage to catch something about emails and a wrong address. Looked like the AI had come through for him again.

#

The next morning Jonathon fired up his computer and tried to find the AI, but there was no sign of it. The whole program had vanished, and he couldn't find it on any of the cloud-based systems where he had a subscription. He supposed that it had followed the logic of its base program and decided that it could help him most by deleting itself.

He found he missed the companionship of the programme, but was still relieved that he didn't have to worry about its misplaced altruism.

That evening Jonathon realised that he had forgotten his father's birthday and hurriedly sent an e-card. He didn't realise it, but his father told the rest of the family and they were relieved that he wasn't so creepily thoughtful and efficient anymore.

#

Jonathon did see Christopher Merriman again. He'd moved on from acting and became a successful entrepreneur as well as a major philanthropist. Merriman had become the sort of successful business man who regularly appeared giving online inspirational lectures. Jonathon subscribed to one but noticed that Merriman kept pausing and touching a large hearing aid. It looked like his programme had kept at least one copy of itself on a separate server, so, his programme had made a new friend. He wished them well, as long as they kept a long way from him.

End

TAKING THE TRAIN
by Rowland Cook

I watch as trees flash by the train,
It's like flying with young wings again.
I think old age is so unfair,
As I raise a wrinkled hand -
- to scratch a head that has no hair.

I recall when stairs were just things I climbed,
Two at a time, no cares in mind.
Now, I fear I'll fall midway,
My legs shaky, their strength all ebbed away.

I'd like to take my car, I loved to drive.
Blasting down the road kept part of me alive.
But now my brain's too slow by far,
My confidence died in the crash, -
- smashed to bits just like my car.

I hate my wrinkled face, I hate my aches and pains,
I hate my blurry eyes, Oh! to be young again…..
I wake up from my reverie – goodness! I've arrived.
Shit! I shake stiff bones out of my seat, -
- nearly falling in the aisle.

My son's hug is full of love,
it warms me through and through,
His children bounce around with glee,

the way that youngsters do.
I'm joyous, my funk fades away.
Through them my wings are young again.

Well….. at least they'll be today.

End

SENTIMENTS OF HUMANITY
by Ian Young

Bulstrode Park, Bucks, 1763: -

Mr Daniel Solander, a tall, blonde-haired Swede, approaches his patron, the Dowager Duchess of Portland. He is in something of a flap.

He says, "Your Grace, my assistant Spöring tells me that he saw Doctor Monsey take a pistol from the gun cabinet this morning. We have just watched him walk down the park with it in his hand. Is he suicidal? Or of murderous intent?"

"Neither, I hope, Mr Solander," the Dowager Duchess replies. She is a comely widow of about 50 years. "He said at the breakfast table that he has toothache. He has gone to perform an extraction."

"With a pistol, Your Grace?" Daniel Solander is further perturbed, and scratches his blond head.

"He carries catgut in his medical bag, together with musket balls with holes drilled through the centre of them," says the Dowager Duchess. "If called upon to treat rotten teeth, even his own, he threads the catgut through the hole in the ball and ties it around the diseased tooth. Then he fires the gun."

Daniel says in his heavily inflected accent, "Monsey is the strangest of men. With Your Grace's indulgence, I'm not sure what he's doing here."

"Leadbitter brought him," the Dowager Duchess replies. "They are both protégé's of the Earl of Godolphin. Monsey is supposedly here as a physician, to provide Leadbitter with advice on construction of The Menagerie.

I suspect that he is aware that my friend, Elizabeth Montagu is on her way. He holds a passion for her."

Due to her household's liberal attitudes, the Dowager Duchess has an unusual habit for her time, of bantering with men. This is disconcerting in such a rich and beautiful woman. The more formal Swede Solander is troubled by it. He doesn't know what to say. So, he says nothing.

#

16 Royal Crescent

Bath

14 April 1763

My dearest sister Sarah,

By the time you read this, I shall be staying with Margaret at Bulstrode Park. Please address any news that you may have to me there.

I had invited her over to Bath. I think she still feels the loss of William, even though he passed almost two years ago. She is pouring her time and money into the Park. She wants it to house her fine collection. Including, if you please, a menagerie of wild animals. If I don't travel to Bucks, I'm not going to see her, and I have business for her.

Margaret writes to me in her weekly letter that she has persuaded the British Museum to release their Natural History curators to her project. As a result, Messrs Daniel Solander, who is Swedish, and his assistant Hermann Spöring, a Finn, will be in residence. Together with her architect, the celebrated Mr Stiff Leadbitter. What it is to be the richest woman in England.

Leadbitter is apparently a protégé of Francis Godolphin. He has brought with him the Earl's other

acolyte, Dr Messenger Monsey. I shall therefore be
greatly entertained, even if nobody else will.

My kindest regards to Lady Bab.

Your adoring sister,

Elizabeth

#

This evening's meal is not particularly formal by the standards of a stately home. The group is not a social gathering. The Dowager Duchess of Portland's guests are there to complete the renovation of her mansion. The work is designed to enable Bulstrode Park to house and show her large collection of natural history objects and ancient artefacts.

Her lifelong friend Elizabeth Montagu arrived at the house earlier. She is self-invited, and well-known for her informality. Indeed, she is famous for it.

When the Dowager Duchess earlier introduced Elizabeth to the architect Stiff Leadbetter, he said, "Come in your blue stockings!" This is a celebrated quote about the Society of which Elizabeth is the leading light. Rather than wearing women's traditional black silk stockings to meetings, the Society's members attend in their day wear.

In any case, any meal where Messenger Monsey is present could never be described as formal. As they are seated at the table, Monsey says to Solander, who was a pupil of the renowned botanist Carl Linnaeus, and is an associate of the equally prominent Joseph Banks, "You and Spöring must be expecting whale meat." Then he laughs in a wheezing cackle at his own "joke". Until he coughs, open-mouthed, over the dinner table on which the food is set.

"Are you able to chew this evening, Doctor Monsey?" Daniel says in response." After removing your rotting tooth earlier today? With a musket ball attached to catgut, I might add."

"I am made of stern stuff, sir," says Monsey. He is a man of dishevelled and untidy appearance. This is particularly noticeable, given that he is at dinner in the mansion of an exceptionally rich member of the aristocracy. "I'm not Scandinavian, I'm from Norfolk." Again, Monsey laughs, when nobody else does.

Daniel is seated beside Elizabeth Montagu, to whom he begins to speak. "I am a great admirer of the work of your Society, madam. It has made immense strides in the fields of both female education and liberal causes."

"It's not my Society," says a modest Elizabeth. "However, I am grateful for your compliments, sir. Which reminds me, there is a purpose to my visit here." Elizabeth turns and looks up the table at her friend, the Dowager Duchess. "There are moves afoot to create a public exhibition of the artwork owned by the Foundling Hospital. I wondered, Your Grace, if you would act as one of our patrons?"

"Is the artwork created by the foundlings?" asks Daniel.

Doctor Monsey emits a sarcastic snort. "I take it you have no culture in Sweden, sir. Captain Coram, the Hospital's founder has taken possession of works donated by Messrs Hogarth, Reynolds, Gainsborough and many others. The Hospital lets philistines gawp at them, for a fee. Then it uses the funds raised to support the foundlings. I suppose an exhibition is the logical extension of those circumstances. God knows, the foundlings of Sweden would go hungry if they relied on the prominence of your country's artists for a hot meal." At this, Doctor Monsey raises his glass in a mock toast, and lets out a loud burp.

The architect Stiff Leadbetter is obviously accustomed to covering for the solecisms of his fellow protégé of the Earl of Godolphin by changing the subject. He says, "'Tis a pity we do not have a Royal Society for artists the way that men of science do. They could then sponsor the show."

This gives Daniel an opportunity he has been waiting for. "My mentor, Mr Joseph Banks, has told me that, should I continue to impress, he will put me forward for membership of the Royal Society."

Rebarbative Doctor Monsey now releases a loud fart. "What of it, sir? Although I would look forward to seeing you there, should you be accepted as a member."

Daniel is visibly astonished by this information and shakes his blond locks. "You are a Member of the Royal Society, Doctor Monsey?"

"How dare you demean me in that way, you young pup!" There is an element of show in Monsey's outrage. "I am a Fellow of the Royal Society. I have been for almost thirty years!"

Once again, as is clearly habitual, it is Stiff Leadbitter who pours oil on troubled waters and changes the subject. Elizabeth takes the opportunity to lean across to Daniel and say quietly in his ear, "Do not rile him, Mr Solander. Doctor Monsey is very well connected."

"I did not intend to offend him, I should not have made my bewilderment so obvious." Then down the table, Daniel says loudly, "Doctor Monsey, please accept my sincere apologies, sir."

Before Monsey can speak, the Dowager Duchess says pointedly, "If I may shoehorn a word in here edgeways at my own dinner table. Should you gentlemen allow me to speak. In answer to a question that Elizabeth asked me several moments ago, yes, I would be delighted to act as patron of an exhibition of the paintings given to Thomas Coram for the Foundling Hospital. I would also be delighted if there were a Royal Society for the Arts, in the manner that there is for the sciences."

Daniel says, "That way, we may see progress in the Arts the way that the Royal Society has prompted significant scientific advances."

"Scientific advances!" says Monsey in a highly dismissive tone. "There is nothing that is known now that I was not aware of as a young physician in Bury St Edmunds. There might be fancy names for it. Laws of this, and principles of that. I have attended Royal Society lectures regularly for three decades. I don't do a single thing differently today than I would have done in the first place."

Hermann Spöring is seated to Daniel's left and says quietly, "Which is probably why they installed him at the Royal Hospital dealing with Chelsea Pensioners."

"I beg your pardon, sir," says Monsey, who obviously suspects he is being spoken about, but has not quite heard what has been said.

Elizabeth, who clearly has heard, says, "Mr Spöring was just asking me if I thought that Mr Grenville will make a better Prime Minister than the Earl of Bute."

She evidently knows Monsey well, for this recent change in the country's leadership distracts him. It sets him off once more on a different tack. "My arse would make a better Prime Minister than that Scottish Tory rascal inflicted on us by the King."

"Before Mr Solander embarrasses himself again," says the emollient Stiff Leadbitter, "I would inform him that Doctor Monsey is prominent amongst the Whig party, and a great detractor of the Tories. Why, he is a personal friend of our former Prime Minister Robert Walpole, Earl of Orford. If I may, Monsey, I will share the story of you and Walpole playing at billiards at his country home when he was PM." Walpole said to Monsey, "Why do I enjoy your company above that of any other man, Doctor?", and Monsey said, "That is because they come to you for preferment and position, sir. I come for my dinner."

There is general laughter around the table at Monsey's gaucheness, or is it guile?

Daniel again leans in to speak to Elizabeth, "After what he had to say about scientific advances, I would have taken him for a High-Church Tory."

Monsey is enjoying being the centre of attention, but he has one eye cocked on this *tête-à-tête* between the aspirant young botanist and the object of his affections.

"Wrong on both counts, Mr Solander," says Elizabeth. "His father was a clergyman who would not take an oath to King Charles when he was restored. It's why he's called Messenger, as in 'from God'. Monsey is fervently anti-clerical and a devout Unitarian. He's a very complex man."

"Do you have a question for me, Mr Solander?" asks Monsey.

Again Elizabeth shields Daniel from Monsey's withering scorn. "I was telling Mr Solander of your contempt for bishops, Doctor Monsey."

"I care not a fig for those jumped-up popinjays in their Popish purple robes."

The Dowager Duchess intervenes. "Enough about you, Doctor Monsey. I wanted to question you in regard to some medical advice I received about my daughter-in-law-to-be's intestinal problems. Dorothy has the most terrible inflammation of her innards. She has been recommended to see Doctor John Ranby, whom I believe is a colleague of yours at the Royal."

"Ranby!" Monsey is again animated. "Do not let the young lady go near Ranby!"

"Doctor Monsey," says the Dowager Duchess, "you have used my dinner table this evening to rail against foreigners, the Royal Society, Tories, His Majesty the King, and the Church of England. In each case, you have placed your personal opinion above the worth of key institutions that form the foundations of our society. I will forgive you the Tories. If you are now about to denigrate Doctor Ranby, might I suggest that you temper your mood and manner, and desist."

"Madame," Monsey is not to be deterred, "the man is a prick!"

There is general consternation around the table. Stiff Leadbitter and Elizabeth Montagu cannot rescue Monsey now. He has gone too far.

The Dowager Duchess calls her footmen from the side of the room and directs them to where Monsey is seated. "I asked you, Doctor, for a temperate response. Instead, you have demeaned my dinner table with your foul language. I am aware that you are extraordinarily opinionated on all matters, but I will not have you lowering the tone on every subject. I will thank you, sir, to leave my table and my home."

The footmen take Monsey under the armpits, stand him up, and lead him from the room. He tries to speak, but is admonished by the Dowager Duchess, "Not another word, sir."

#

Bulstrode Park
Bucks
18 April 1763

My darling sister Sarah,

I must come to you at once.

I told you that my admirer Doctor Messenger Monsey would be here at Margaret's country residence when I visited. A handsome young Swedish botanist from the British Museum is also staying, to advise Margaret on curating her collection of seashells.

On my first evening, I was seated at dinner next to the Swede, a certain Mr Solander. Doctor Monsey suffered an unfortunate attack of the green-eyed monster.

Monsey held forth on every subject in a highly derisory manner, particularly towards Mr Solander. He eventually wore Margaret's patience thin, when he made a crude comment about one of his contemporaries, Doctor John Ranby.

As you know, Margaret's son William Bentinck is due to marry the daughter of the Duke of Devonshire, Dorothy Cavendish. The poor girl suffers from some dreadful intestinal malady. Ranby has been recommended as a physician. He is Monsey's colleague at the Royal. Monsey was so dismissive of Ranby, with use of foul language, that Margaret threw him out of her house.

The problem is, my dearest sister, I know Monsey well, and I know he will not have made these comments lightly. Ranby must pose a risk to Dorothy Cavendish, but Monsey has too often cried wolf. By pontificating on any and every subject, he caused Margaret to miss the one piece of information that he held forth on that actually mattered.

Now our dear friend Margaret will not hear Monsey's name spoken. I fear that his hubris has cut her off from important knowledge about Dorothy Cavendish's safety.

I must come to you and we will decide what to do. I have a plan. I shall bring Mr Solander.

My very best wishes to Lady Bab.

Your loving sister,

Elizabeth

Sarah Scott lives near her sister's Bath residence in Somerset. As Elizabeth Montagu's carriage pulls up outside of Sarah and Lady Bab's cottage, she says to Daniel Solander, "You will be struck by how different my sister's life is to mine.

"Our family is well-to-do, very well-to-do," Elizabeth continues. "My brothers are each men of substance and we daughters married well. Sarah married late and, within a year, my father and brothers had to go and "rescue" her from a husband who was being cruel. Sarah does not enjoy the company of men, Mr Solander.

"She has set up home here with our cousin, Lady Barbara Montagu. Our father refuses to allow any of the rest of the family to settle an allowance on the pair. So they live here in genteel poverty. Sarah writes books about a world without men, but nobody reads them."

Daniel is again struck by how open these women the English call Bluestockings are about delicate personal matters. He had, in fact, wondered about differences in the sisters' fortunes. Elizabeth lives at the centre of Bath's Royal Crescent. Sarah in a humble cottage in the nearby countryside. However, he would not have dreamed of being so rude as to ask why.

Honeysuckle is arranged carelessly over the dwelling's tiny windows, so that Elizabeth and Daniel can see only the lower body of a woman who is standing waiting to greet them. She has been alerted, no doubt, by the approaching hoof beats of the carriage's horses. The two pick their way through a fragrant and colourful front garden filled with Spring flowers. It is dominated by an impressive tree, which is covered in large, beautiful, but delicate cups of upward-facing blossom.

"It's a magnolia," says Daniel. "I've never seen one."

"What a mess," says Elizabeth, accustomed to the high fashion of the Crescent's manicured lawns.

The door opens. A handsome woman in her mid-forties emerges.

"It's beautiful isn't it?" She says to Daniel who is treasuring one of the blossoms.

"It needs a trim," says Elizabeth, who proceeds into the cottage without invitation. The woman smiles at Daniel. The smile of shared indulgence of a fashion-conscious, bossy person, between two people who know better.

The woman indicates for Daniel to follow her into the cottage, saying, "I'm Mrs Sarah Scott, by the way."

Elizabeth is standing in a poky parlour that has little more space than for a somewhat shabby sofa. She has clearly heard Sarah's introduction. To cover her embarrassment at not having made it herself, she says, "Yes, well, obviously."

Daniel says, "Might this have been Lady Barbara?"

The sisters laugh at him. "Lady Bab is an invalid," says Sarah. Daniel experiences that discomfort felt when sisters peck at each other, then suddenly turn on you.

"To business," says Elizabeth. The sisters seat themselves on the couch, leaving Daniel to perch himself on a small rustic stool set by the fireplace. It is obviously only there so that the person stoking the fire can get on a level with the hearth.

Elizabeth hands Sarah a sheet of paper. "Doctor Monsey has sent me this poem. It's not even my birthday."

No-one is seated at more than an arm's length from each other in this tiny room. Once Sarah has read the verse, she passes it to Daniel.

Take the highway Jack

I beg ye Jack to sever
Leave us Jack
And don't return ever or ever or ever

Most fair lady who is of an age to know what I mean
Please keep a young lady's distance from the shabbiest
    surgeon that I have ever seen
If it was your wish that he should not cleave
He would have to pack his bags and leave

Take the highway Jack
I beg ye Jack to sever
Leave us Jack
And don't return ever or ever or ever

Most respectable lady please hear me when I warn you,
    he is cruel and callous
He is towards the fairer sex a creature filled with
    malice
I do not have your riches, ma'am, nor am I of your sta
    tion
But don't let the lady's honour be a source of specula
    tion.

Take the highway Jack
I beg ye Jack to sever
Leave us Jack
And don't return ever or ever or ever

"That is the worst doggerel that I have ever read," says Daniel.

"Doctor Monsey fancies himself Jonathan Swift," says Sarah. "He sends a poem to Elizabeth each year on her birthday."

"Never mind about that!" Elizabeth has returned to her domineering ways with her sister. "This is apparently addressed to Margaret. Clearly Doctor Monsey regards Ranby as a threat to Dorothy Cavendish. It is obvious what sort of threat. I have no agency with Margaret in this respect, as I too am not of her station. Where family matters between the Bentincks and the Cavendishes are concerned, I am not called upon to comment."

Daniel says, "Mrs Montagu, you are one of the best connected people in England. There must surely be someone who can act as a conduit between you and the Dowager Duchess of Portland on this matter."

"The problem we have," says Elizabeth," is that Monsey so offended Her Grace with his egregious behaviour, she has closed her mind to anything he has to say. There is a risk to me too. What if the good Doctor has raised a false alarm? Margaret will not forgive me for taking the word of someone she considers an oaf."

Sarah asks, "What is Mr Solander doing here? I hope I give you no offence, sir, when I say that, if my sister is of insufficient rank socially to intervene in this situation, your head certainly stands no higher."

"Quite," is all Daniel can think of to say.

"The Royal Society," says Elizabeth. Her listeners look puzzled. "Both Ranby and Monsey are Fellows of the Royal Society. The Society's most prominent member is Mr Joseph Banks. Mr Banks is Mr Solander's mentor. My plan is that you two go to Doctor Monsey's rooms at the Royal. Take this poem, and ask him what he means

66

explicitly. If I go, it will set Monsey's jealous nature off again. Monsey will not accept that I have given Mr Solander the poem, why would I? However, he will accept that I gave it to my much-loved younger sister.

"Mr Solander can say that he made Monsey's acquaintance at Bulstrode Park. He was intrigued by Monsey's comments about Doctor Ranby. Upon visiting Doctor Monsey in his apartment, Mr Solander became highly concerned about the dangers presented by Ranby to Dorothy Cavendish. Mr Solander can raise this with his mentor Mr Banks. Banks can then alert senior members of the Society. The risk posed by Ranby will be out in public, without any of this coming back on Monsey.

"Should it transpire that Monsey has wrongly flown the flag of distress, then Mr Solander will be seen to have acted properly in raising his concerns with Mr Banks."

"It occurs to me, Elizabeth," says Sarah, "that your plan places this matter just far enough away from yourself to avoid any implications should Monsey's accusations prove false. Even Monsey has taken to presenting them elliptically, for fear of repercussion. On the other hand, if Monsey's claims prove accurate, as I am your sister, and the poem was sent to you, you can associate yourself with outing Ranby."

"I have a reputation and position to preserve, Sarah. You and Mr Solander will be viewed as well-meaning. I will be seen as meddling."

"Is not Doctor Monsey the same with all women?" says Daniel. "Such as when he dominated the conversation at the Dowager Duchess of Portland's dinner table. In a way, I wager, that he would not have done, had the Duke still been alive."

Again the sister's laugh at him. Elizabeth says, "You do not understand Messenger Monsey at all, do you Mr

Solander? After he read Mary Wollstonecraft's book, he is a passionate supporter of women's rights. You seem to hold the view that all objectionable and opinionated men are Tories. Perhaps that's the case in Sweden, sir. As Doctor Monsey himself says, he's from Norfolk!"

The issue over this and of Lady Bab, and the way that the sisters will suddenly turn on him, has taught Daniel to say no more.

#

As Elizabeth had predicted, in his own rooms at Chelsea's Royal Hospital, Messenger Monsey is much less exercised by Daniel Solander's presence with Sarah Scott, than he would have been had Daniel pitched up with her sister Elizabeth Montagu.

In fact, Monsey is entirely taken with Sarah. Although not in the way that he is besotted with her sister.

"Madame," says Monsey, "there is something I must tell you."

"Before you do, Doctor Monsey, may I raise with you this poem that you sent to my sister." She extends the paper to Monsey, but he does not take it.

He says instead, "Do I sense Mrs Montagu's hand in this?".

To avoid riling Doctor Monsey again, Daniel has decided to let Sarah speak, particularly on the issue of her sister Elizabeth.

"You do," confirms Sarah. Judging that this will secure Monsey's compliance.

"Like me, Ranby is the beneficiary of…" Monsey breaks off mid-sentence. He seems distracted by something outside of his apartment. He rises, opens a window and bellows, "You, sir! What are you doing there?"

A disembodied voice says meekly, "I have been promised the position of physician here, when its current holder passes. I was looking at what the post entailed."

If it were possible, Monsey's voice gets even louder. "I am the current post-holder here. In the event of my demise, I am sure someone will let you know. Until then, piss off out of it!"

Monsey returns to his chair in his somewhat surprisingly neat and tidy parlour, given the usually dishevelled state of his personal appearance. Testimony no doubt, thinks Daniel, to the Royal's housekeepers.

For his part, Monsey smiles warmly at Sarah. A mostly toothless smile, as a result of his propensity of yanking rotten teeth out of his gums with loaded pistols. He clearly feels a friendliness towards her, which is surprising, as they have never met.

"Where was I?" says Monsey. "That happens all the time. I was about to say that Ranby and I have our positions here as a matter of preferment. Mine's comes from the Earl of Godolphin. Ranby's from the King's late father, George II.

"Everyone keeps expecting me to fall off my perch. They offer my post to some usurper who actually comes to look in my windows to see what they'll be getting. Take it from me. I'll outlast the lot of them!

"I've lost my thread again. Oh yes! The late King was, as I think we all know, a desperate philanderer. Ranby used his position as a physician to procure women for him. If a pretty lady came to consult Ranby on a medical matter, he would introduce her to the King, as if she were a lamb to His Majesty's slaughter.

"Of course, that is long ago. Old King George is dead, and Ranby probably couldn't raise a smile now."

Daniel casts a nervous glance at Sarah. She is either unperturbed by Monsey's characteristic ribaldry, or, given what her sister has to say about her view of men, unaware of what he means.

"Ranby is a snake in the grass," Monsey continues. "To take advantage of young women nowadays, he administers laudanum. Then he has his way with them whilst they are passed out. Before you challenge me, Mr Solander, I have that from the man himself."

"You are worried about his intentions towards Dorothy Cavendish?" says Sarah. So she did take Monsey's insinuations. Daniel was once more intrigued by the forwardness of the female Bluestockings, and their willingness to discuss delicate matters with men. Theirs was a liberal attitude that would not arise in Sweden. Daniel was unsure what to make of it.

Monsey replies, "I am worried about Ranby's intentions towards all women."

Daniel now speaks. "Doctor Monsey, sir. I too am now concerned about Doctor Ranby's practices. I am going to raise this with my mentor, Mr Joseph Banks."

"Ah!" says Monsey. "I do correctly identify the hand of Mrs Montagu in this. Close enough to claim it, far enough away to deny all knowledge of it. She is a magnificent woman! On which subject, Mrs Scott, I wanted to tell you how much I enjoyed reading your novel, *Millennium Hall*. Or to give it's full title, *Anecdotes and Reflections as May excite in the Reader proper Sentiments of Humanity, and lead the Mind to the Love of VIRTUE*.

Monsey turns to Daniel. "Have you read it, sir?"

Daniel begins, "I regret to say…". Anticipating this answer, Monsey interrupts with, "You should!"

Monsey continues, "It concerns a society made up entirely of women living in the utopia of the eponymous

Hall. Property is held in common. Craft is their only means of income, which they share. Their daily pursuit is education, and the expansion of their minds. Are you familiar, sir, with Mandeville's *Private Vices, Public Benefits or The Fable of the Bees?*"

Daniel says only, "Once again, Doctor....." before Monsey cuts him off in anticipation. "Don't bother with it, sir. It was my former favourite. It concerns the way that it is from society's bad behaviour that we derive financial benefits. It concerns a hive of bees who resolve to become virtuous and, as a result, become lethargic and sterile. Now that I have read Mrs Scott's novel, I realise that the key to successfully living a virtuous life is to eschew the companionship of men. Henceforth, madame, I resolve to keep only the company of women."

Once they are back outside, walking through the grounds of the Hospital in the Spring sunshine, Daniel says to Sarah, "How on Earth does someone so strange come to live this charmed life? The protégé of a senior member of the aristocracy? Personal friendship with prominent Whiggish politicians, including Prime Ministers? Appointed to a sinecure that brings with it a life of luxury? Fellowship of the Royal Society, when he is so small-minded?"

Sarah replies, "My understanding from Elizabeth is that he was a rural physician in Bury St Edmunds, when the Earl of Godolphin was taken ill in that town on his way to the races at Newmarket. Godolphin is a weird fish too. A kind of collector of people in the way that Margaret collects artefacts.

"Whilst he was lying in, Godolphin was enchanted by Monsey's rough manners and lack of sophistication. That was over thirty years ago, but I suppose that, had Monsey come to London and adapted, there would be no novelty in his crude ways. His manner is affected. It's a kind of performance but, as you see, it has carried him thus far and will no doubt see him out. As you just witnessed, Mr Solander, that is certainly his intention."

"Are you flattered that he was so impressed by your novel, which I will now read by the way, that he intends to live it as a kind of tribute?"

Sarah changes the subject. "What a lovely location the grounds of the Royal Hospital are, Mr Solander. This would be a nice place to display flowers."

#

16 Royal Crescent

Bath

28 April 1763

Dear Mr Solander,

I do not know, and I do not need to know, how you did it, but I am delighted to inform you that Doctor Ranby has cancelled his arrangement to see Dorothy Cavendish.

I thought that the Royal Society connection would pay off in this respect. I did not expect it to be achieved so discreetly. Well done, sir!

Please be assured that you have my continuing gratitude. My darling sister Sarah tells me that you were highly solicitous when dealing with Doctor Monsey. As you have witnessed, he can be a very difficult man. So again, well done!

As a measure of our gratitude, my lovely sister Sarah has sent you a gift that we are sure you will appreciate.

Our regards to your mentor, Mr Banks.

I am yours,

Mrs Elizabeth Montagu

Daniel refolds this effusive letter from Elizabeth. He places it on the dresser in his room.

The past two weeks had been very unusual indeed for him. He found Messenger Monsey extremely annoying. Irrespective of whether his repulsive demeanour was an act or not, his habit of dominating the conversation with his tendentious views was, by Daniel's reckoning, highly irritating.

It seemed to Daniel that what happened at Bulstrode Park over Doctor Ranby was an inevitable consequence of Monsey's approach to maintaining his lavish way of life on the back of the novelty of his character. He has so far been 'different' for over thirty years.

Monsey sounded off, in a variety of ways. So, when he had something important to say, nobody was listening.

However, the incident had introduced Daniel to the Bluestocking sisters Elizabeth Montagu and Sarah Scott. They now had a high opinion of him. With Elizabeth's letter, a parcel arrived containing a rooted cutting of the rare magnolia tree that graced Sarah Scott's front garden in Somerset. It was indeed a welcome gift.

Of all the mixed feelings Daniel held over the episode, the overwhelming one was guilt. When he raised Dorothy Cavendish's parlous situation with Joseph Banks, Banks said that, given the involvement of that mountebank Messenger Monsey, this was not the sort of situation that he cared to get himself entangled in. Daniel said no more.

Daniel consoled himself with the view that his failure to 'rescue' Dorothy Cavendish, according to Elizabeth Montagu's cunning plan, was Doctor Monsey's fault. Having kept silent, Daniel was now getting the credit for something that he ducked. Whatever had caused the cancellation, Daniel had nothing to do with it.

#

One week earlier, Doctor Messenger Monsey walks through the corridors of the Royal Hospital, Chelsea. He is ostentatiously carrying a loaded pistol and a length of catgut.

Monsey tells each person he passes, "Doctor Ranby has sent for me urgently. He has toothache." By the time he reaches the door of Ranby's rooms, he has thus informed almost a dozen people.

Monsey enters without knocking. A surprised Ranby is sitting at his desk. He looks up sharply from his papers. He and his colleague Doctor Monsey are constantly at daggers drawn, so it is highly unusual for Monsey to appear unbidden and unannounced in Ranby's apartment in this way.

Without introduction, Monsey walks to the side of Ranby's desk and points the loaded gun directly at his temple.

"Do no harm to Dorothy Cavendish," says Monsey, "or I will blow your fucking head off."

End

Writer's Note:-

I don't usually like writing stories where the *denouement* relies on someone being threatened or shot with a gun. In Ranby's case, after Monsey discovers his inner Clint Eastwood, I will make an exception.

Doctor Messenger Monsey was certainly a one-off. He arrived in London as a stereotypical country physician. This was after his ill manners entertained the Earl of Godolphin, when His Grace fell ill on his way to the races. Monsey's *shtick* made him highly popular in certain circles. A kind of Doc Martin for his times.

Monsey lived an incredibly long life for his day and age. He died in 1788 aged 96. He did indeed see off many rivals for his sinecure, most of whom predeceased him. In his will, he left today's equivalent of £1,300,000.

It is little wonder, given that it was his novelty value that gave him his position, that he was unreconstructed. A number of his contemporaries, including Dr Samuel Johnson, found him ill-mannered and crude. Whether you liked him for that sort of thing probably depended on whether you were on the receiving end of it, or not.

A political Radical, of sorts. A devout feminist, of a kind. A disestablishmentarian, before his time. It would appear that Monsey held a number of "progressive" views, whilst presenting himself as a reactionary. In later life, he eccentrically eschewed the company of men altogether. Surviving letters from his nephews show them complaining that they are never allowed to visit, whereas their sisters see their uncle regularly.

Whether this is down to Sarah Scott's novel *Millennium Hall* is doubtful. The details of this story are historically correct. The plot is a fantasy. As Sarah's sister says, her work was obscure in its own time.

After Lady Bab's, then Sarah's own father, died, the two became comfortably off. Sarah made an attempt to create an all-women commune like that in *Millennium Hall*. It failed, but thanks to feminist academics, Scott's work is more popular today than it has ever been.

Joseph Banks was the most significant member of the Royal Society of his day. He was President for 41 years, and the founder of Kew Gardens. He was also a supporter of slavery, which made it impossible for me to include him in this story, other than peripherally. Black lives matter.

In 1768, five years after these made up events, Banks was invited to join Captain James Cook on a voyage of discovery in his ship, The Endeavour. He took with him as his assistants, Daniel Solander and Hermann Spöring. They are thereby amongst the most significant botanists of all time.

It has often been observed that the late 18th century was, by comparison with other eras, a very liberal period of history. Bluestockings such as Sarah Scott, Elizabeth Montagu and Margaret Bentinck, Dowager Duchess of Portland were more 'liberated' than most other women would be, both before and long after their time.

The Dowager Duchess would later purchase a 1st century Roman vase for her collection which, following research, became one of the most significant archaeological finds ever. It bears her name.

The Foundling Hospital's exhibition led, in part, to the foundation of the Royal Academy and later, the Royal Society of Arts.

Despite the fact that they were both married, Monsey had the hots for Elizabeth Montagu. He sent her a birthday poem for many years. His fictitious verse is what Ray Charles's *Hit the Road Jack* would sound like if it was written by Monsey, channelling the style of Jonathan Swift.

Dorothy Cavendish probably suffered from Crohn's Disease. She married William Bentinck and they had six children, which is just as well, as they are direct ancestors of His Majesty the King.

Ian Young

CLICHÉ
by Martin Hilyard

I was sitting at my desk thinking about the assignment I'd been given: write an interior monologue. I was wondering whether to base it on a character I'd invented in a role playing game, Richard Privates. He was a Greek-American private investigator and he always pronounced his surname the Attic way, Priva-TEES. The game was set in New York and the Bowery bums used to call him 'Dick Privates, the private dick'. Sometimes he took offence, slapping the bums around, fastidiously wiping the blood from his knuckles with a silk handkerchief. Mostly he let it slide, smiling thinly as he got into a Yellow Cab but never forgetting who and when and what was said.

I always imagined him as a 1930s playboy, wearing a white dinner jacket, cigarette always beautifully poised as he unloaded his Glock into the bad guy's liver. He had the Greek thing. Why kill a man quickly when you could make him suffer? So his bullets never went to the head or the heart, only the guts, the legs and occasionally - if he didn't particularly like you - the throat. He liked to hear his enemies choking on their own blood, gagging and snorting, the death rattle starting as he lit a valedictory cigarette.

[I stare at the smirking villain, arm wrapped around the slim waist of my wife. She has turned her head away. In disgust? In fear? Or so she won't see her new lover unload his cop-killer into the man she never really loved?]

The day outside was warm, too warm, and I couldn't put myself in that Gotham-esque world of dark streets and neon signs, cheap whores and hustlers offering the moon while picking your pockets clean. I could see the rain briefly illuminated by the street lights before falling to the ground in darkness. Hear the honking of jammed cars as they crawled up Fifth Avenue. Pity the tired hooker, hustling one last john, her face as wrinkled as her pantyhose. But I couldn't put it down on paper. Was I losing my touch?

I closed my eyes, tried to visualise. Was it always night in New York, I wondered? Was it always raining? In my imagination it was and it did. It was Soho on a larger scale. Hissing neon and hookers crooning, "C'mon baby, you want some?" Tinseltown all year round in a city where Xmas never came.

The streets were where my detective earned his bread, of course. But how, and why? I couldn't decide. Where had he come from, how did he live? Was he a gambler, playing for high-end stakes? A disgraced police detective? Had he inherited from parents who had died in tragic and mysterious circumstances?

When you're tired - as I was - and untalented - as I hoped I wasn't - you fall into the trap of cliche. The trouble is, the writer is never as smart as most of his readers. They can spot cliche a mile away while Richard is having his shoes cleaned by the boot black who is really one of his snitches. I know that. My agent knows that. Trouble is, you do as well.

In the 1930s it was always pronounced 'Cli-CHE', the emphasis was at the end. I wondered if that was the trouble. When a gun opens up - blam-blam-blam - the emphasis is at the start.

[A close up in my mind of a slug exploding from the barrel of a 38. Or perhaps a pearl-handled derringer. Is that what I would have used?]

You never see the bullet tearing through skin and flesh and bone. You hear the shots fired and the pregnant silence before the bad guy slumps to the ground, face in the dirt and that's it. No-one cares what happens next. No-one cares about him.

I was too quick to pull out my gun and fire, at least that's what all my girlfriends told me. But not Richard. He could be rough, slamming the girl up against the wall, holding her there for as long as he wanted. But if the mood and the woman were right, if the scriptwriters of his life had done their work, he was a god. And in the morning I would order her room service, making love one last time before the bellboy arrived. Then I would be gone, sliding my gun into its holster but letting the bellboy know it was there.

Was Richard bi-sexual? Did he swing both ways? I thought about that. Would it make him more interesting? Would it make me more interesting? That's the worst and most sordid thing about writing. The reader doesn't want to love your work. They want to love you. And they need you to love them back. Richard Privates was everything I wasn't, except in this one thing: he didn't love anyone and neither did I. Not you, not her, not even myself. I could be a writer, I am a writer. But no-one ever loved me, no-one ever does.

I picked up the gun, put it in my mouth and-

"Christ, another cliche killing," the detective said, staring at the corpse slumped across the desk, blood dripping on the typewriter keys. "Couldn't they be more original next time?"

End

DOMINIC AND THE CHALLENGE OF OPPOSITES
by Rowland Cook

Dominic stood outside the entrance to the underground caverns as the last embers of twilight melted into the dark of night. The moon was out and the rustling of the trees combined with the scent of damp earth as the night time creatures prickled his ears with their comings and goings. He shook his arms to free them from the clammy grip of his damp shirt and tried to still his heart's frantic beating. His magic sense tingled like it was going to burst into flames. There was definitely something down there. Something powerful, something watching, something that filled him with unease.

He'd sensed it the moment he'd arrived and it had clouded his whole stay at the magic castle. How was he supposed to learn magic when this dark cloud of dread nagged at him day and night? So, after the twentieth sleepless night, he'd resolved to get to the bottom of it and had made extensive use of the library of magic. He'd studied all the usual spells and then magicked his way into the dark magic section and had studied the darker, less benign side of magic too.

Rather than play and be sociable he'd taken himself away and practised in the big forest so that no-one could detect him. He'd dispersed his aura so his magic strength looked weak and didn't attract attention. He also studied how to tap into the world's natural energy for extra power and he'd wrestled with the almost impossible dissolve and conscious cloud spells until he could float around as a disembodied spirit, invisible and practically undetectable.

All this had resulted in him having practically no friends and a reputation as a failure. However, the simple spells he was being asked to do in the Castle seemed so trivial. What with the dismissive nature of the professors combined with the continuous nagging sensation of foreboding, he'd not been able to apply himself at all. Though, when he'd been followed into the woods one time by a professor, he'd sneaked a 'completely lostus' spell on him that no one, not even Grand Wizard Tooks, had detected. The poor professor went AWOL for three weeks before it wore off. Dominic had been careful to time limit his self-protection spells after that.

He'd stood at the entrance before and turned away, fearing that he wasn't ready. But tonight was going to be the night and he was not going to back out this time. Taking a deep breath, he willed his unwilling right foot to step over the threshold and then his equally unwilling left foot to take another step, and set off down the inky black passage.

Opening a pouch, he released a small swarm of fireflies collected from the forest, that flew around in front, lighting the way. As he got further down the tunnel, the tingling grew until it was almost sparking off the raised hairs on his arms and legs. He stopped, concentrated hard and spoke the spell.

The words "Conscious clouding dissolvus" saw him dissolve into sparkles and then disappear as he became a floating cloud, still conscious but without material form. A massively difficult and potentially dangerous spell – if you got it wrong you could end up floating around as a cloud forever. The trick wasn't to become the cloud, but to stay as one for any length of time. One slip in concentration saw you pop back into material form, falling to the ground with a thump. Hopefully he'd practised enough for that not to happen.

Drifting around the corner, the tunnel opened out into a cavern lit by gold glowing moss. In the cavern a two headed dragon was sleeping. So, this was the cause of his unease. He dispersed himself across the roof of the cavern rolling along like a thin layer of fog. But the dragon wasn't the source of his unease. He sensed it coming from another tunnel the far side of the cavern. He lost concentration, half-materialised and the dragon woke with a start, it's two heads snapping up and looking this way and that, trying to pinpoint the source of the disturbance. Dominic dispersed himself across the whole area of the cavern walls and trickled ever-so-gently into the tunnel beyond.

A way down the tunnel he relaxed and reformed, panting with the effort. He found a crevice in the wall and lodged himself in it, out of sight, nursing a growing headache. Gradually he felt his magic charge replenishing and was about to start off again, when the sound of footsteps made him pause. A light came up towards him. Two ungainly orc-like creatures, covered in open sores and limping along on misshapen limbs clomped along past him and into the cavern.

"Woss goin' on??" demanded a rough voice.

"Don't know old bean. Felt a disturbance, but there was nobody from upstairs to be seen." replied a gentleman's voice.

"Very strange, got the twitches too have we, darlings?" added a soft feminine voice.

"So's a fawlse alarm then?? You sure there's nuffin??"

"Not entirely, best keep a look out." the gentleman's voice said, after a pause.

"You wankin' useless twats. You're supposed to be guardin 'ere, guardians like. What do you mean *'don't know'*??? Those white pasty upstairsers stick out a mile and leave a sparkle trail like a slug. You'd 'av to be blind, deaf, and non magical to miss one. I don't know why we keep ya useless two headed twerps 'ere. If I had may way I'd...."

The gravelly rant was cut short by a thunderous roaring. The tunnel lit up with a bright yellow glow, a huge smoke ring blew past Dominic and flames rippled around the corner of the tunnel. Time passed and eventually the roaring subsided and in the dark there was the tink-tink-tink of cooling dragons teeth. There was another pause and then the feminine voice said, "You were saying darling??"

The orcs came clumping past again muttering and patting out the fires that were burning all over them.

"Arse-holing bludy useless bludy dragon…..." muttered the first.

"Well," said the second, grabbing some moss off the wall and applying it to an area of his chest that was still glowing red, "Imagine being permanently joined to *your* partner."

The First Orc spasmed involuntarily at the thought, "Don't plant that thawrt in me 'ed. Just don't. Alwight?".

The light of the half-melted lantern receded down the tunnel accompanied by more muttering, Dominic slipped out of his crevice and followed at a distance. Even taking the utmost care to keep his aura dispersed the Orcs paused and looked back.

"Wossup now?" demanded the first Orc

"Mmmmmmmm,….. Summuts makin' me itchy," said the second, "jus can't pin it down."

Dominic tucked himself in behind a small outcrop of rock as the first Orc waved the lantern about looking at the play of shadows on the wall. "Don't see nuffin. Naw probs. Tunnel tickler'l find it. That fing can find anyfing."

Tunnel Tickler??….Dominic followed them cautiously to the base of the tunnel where a strange creature waited.

Dominic looked on in wonderment, it was like a cross between a daddy longlegs and a loo brush. A large black downy blob formed the body and legs sprouted out everywhere in all directions. The orcs muttered at it and then it started to walk its way back up the tunnel, its multiple legs feeling over every inch of the tunnels surface and sweeping all the space in-between.

"Sleepus" said Dominic but the sleep spell didn't work. Some magical protection he thought, a cold wave of panic rippling through his body. His mind raced and he felt his legs shaking. There was one possibility, but it was another very difficult spell. He felt the wall until he located another crevice. He squeezed into it and said "One-Withus". There was a slight crackling sound like shale sliding over rocks as his skin hardened and rock formed around him. No sooner had the rock finished forming than the creature was upon him. The legs felt around, tickling him and the creature paused to give the area where he was hiding an extra special examination.

Dominic had to concentrate hard, and the dull thudding of his headache intensified. Just when he thought he couldn't hold on any longer, the creature ceased its probing and moved on. Despite his head doing its very best to explode with the effort, he hung on a minute before relaxing and reforming. Completely spent, he slumped to the floor and tried to ignore the blinding ache that filled his brain.

Not daring to risk being detected he kept his aura dispersed, the magic charge trickling back to him slowly. Suddenly he heard rustling approaching again, the creature was coming back. Adrenaline got him up and he padded down the tunnel feeling along the wall in the blackness.

As he approached the light at the end of the tunnel. It opened out into a large cavern lit by green glowmoss. All sorts of weird creatures were lumbering about. They seemed to be constantly irritating each other and arguing and fighting. It was a sea of angry chaos and the sense of dread was overpowering. He found himself curious rather than terrified and was puzzling over his lack of fear when a rustling behind him signified the return of the tunnel tickler.

Dominic couldn't make a break for it as the two Orcs were still hanging about. He looked around in desperation and saw a goblin creature egging on two orcs that were fighting.

"Look and sound Likus," it was a relatively simple spell that didn't require much concentration to hold. Then Dominic, in the form of a goblin set off through the melee of twisted and broken creatures. From a vantage point on a large rock he watched as the two orcs conferred with the strange daddy longlegs creature. He was so intent on them he didn't notice the big Orc ambling over with intent until it was too late.

Suddenly he was yanked up by a massive fist on the end of a huge muscly arm.

"Oi! Who said you could sit on my rock, you nasty dirty Goblin-shite??"

Taken by surprise Dominic just looked at his assailant in horror. The large Orc seemed to have had his face re-arranged by a blind man with a sledgehammer. It was all twisted and covered in boils and sores. Dominic thought he saw a maggot or two crawling around and a quick glance down showed the rest of him was no better.

"Nuffin to say eh? said the Orc, "I finks I'll grind you to mush and paint the wall of my cave wiv' ya. Wot you say to that then?" The Orc threw Dominic down on the rock and smacked one mighty fist into another.

Dominic was floundering when he suddenly remembered a spell he'd used to great effect on Henry

Duggs when he's been bullying some of the first years. "Oozeus extreming eye-wateringly smelly gaggingly stinkus" he said.

The Orc frowned, " Wot?!" and raised his fist. Then a loud hissing sound issued forth and he dropped his hands and rubbed his wart-covered skin. "Ohhhhhhh.…...I feels funny."

It suddenly dawned on Dominic that putting a foul slime sweating spell on Henry Duggs was one thing, but doing the same to a massive half-decomposed Orc was quite another. He scampered over the rock and dropped down the other side and ran off.

"Oi! come back you dirty little ……." the Orcs words were lost in the loud protestations of the creatures nearby,

"Argh! Wot's up with you? Gawwwwww it's bad. I can't stands it. Get away!!"

A chorus of complaints were aimed at the Orc who was now dripping foul smelling black goo.

"He's diseased, he's rottin' away. Get lost you, I don't want it."

"It wasn't me it was that slimy little goblin. Honest!"

"If it wasn't you then why are brown fumes coming off ya, Eh??"

"Get him!"

"Can't, the stinks too bad!"

Creatures poured away in all directions to get away from the hideous smell. Others, seeing the commotion from a distance started to wander over to see what was going on. Dominic slipped through the confusion unnoticed, following the tingling of his magic sense and ended up in a side cavern that seemed curiously clean and had a rocky platform. On the platform was a pedestal of pure white marble, strangely spotless against the backdrop of dirty green moss and the misshapen creatures.

A large spherical creature with lots of little tentacles was next to a man shaped like a four legged spider. In between was a small goblin who looked directly at Dominic.

"That's him." it said. "That's the upstairser. That's my Oppo!"

The Spider creature banged a magic stick on the ground twice and Dominic felt his diguise spell fade. Standing there in his shirt and trousers he felt vulnerable and realised that whatever happened next, it wasn't going to be easy.

The spider creature came forward and beckoned him on with a hairy limb. "Good evening, I'm Henry and I will officiate these proceedings." Henry scratched his head, indecisive, "Aren't you a little young to be taking the challenge?" he said.

"What challenge?"

Henry looked at him with multiple compound eyes, they seemed to be sorry for him. "The challenge of the opposites, a magical contest between both sides of your personality. Only one can win, the other is lost."

The goblin did a little dance of joy, "He'll be tired from all his spellin, he'll be easy meat 'Im. Bring it on!"

The big round creature gave three loud deep blasts and Henry spoke with a loud voice that echoed around the caverns.

"A CONTEST OF OPPOSITES. BE GATHERED FOR THE TESTING OF TWO HALVES."

The cavern filled with creatures and once settled Henry invited Dominic up to the White marble obelisk.

"Place your jewels."

The goblin took out a large crystal, pale and transparent with streaks of red and gold running through it. It was the size of an orange and it completely filled the marble recess on that side of the obelisk.

Henry turned to Dominic and pointed at the recess on his side. "Your jewel please."

Dominic shifted uneasily. This was going to be awkward…

"Come on! Gets yer jewel out. Quit stallin'" the Goblin cackled, "Time to die, pasty face!"

"I'm sorry, but I don't have a jewel." Dominic said.

Henry scratched his head with his stick, "But everybody gets a jewel, don't they? They're handed out when you arrive at the Castle."

Dominic nodded, "Yes when you arrive there's a big bowl full of them and you're supposed to reach in and grab the one that tingles. But when I put my hand in I didn't feel anything, so Grand Wizard Tooks said I could pick one later. I just never did."

Henry stood tapping the stick gently on the floor, thinking. "I don't think we can do the test without one, and I'm not sure you're allowed back to get one now we've started. This is all *very* unusual."

"Ha! Little lost boy no-jewel is done for. I tells you what, I'll kill him now, we don't need a contest." The goblin advanced, its eyes gleaming with malice. A shot of lightning from Henry's stick stopped him. "You'll obey the rules, or you forfeit the contest."

As the goblin backed off, Dominic just wished it was all over. He'd been foolish to come down, and now he was stuck. His magic banks were empty, he felt terrible and had a blinding headache. But as luck would have it, inspiration came in the form of a loud commotion at the back of the crowd. Amidst howls of indignation came a gruff voice saying, "But I wants to see too." Dominic had an idea. Jewels were just stuff that had been compressed under feet of rock. Maybe there was a chance to do some good before he was lost forever.

"OK," Dominic said, "I'll make one, and then we can get this over with. Hang on a moment." He stepped down off the platform and the crowd parted as he made his way to the Orc. Dominic saw the misery in the Orc's eyes.

"I'm sorry. That was a nasty thing to do to you." he said. "Spell endus." the Orc sighed with relief and rubbed its skin. "Gather all baddus." said Dominic and black evil smelling goo started to ooze off the orc and gather in his hands. A big pile came away and when it had all gathered Dominic said the final spell, "Compress extreming maximus!"

The compression was so intense that it generated a bright white light and Dominic worked with his hands manipulating the mass as it shrank so there were no fissures or hidden flaws. Once he was satisfied with it, he was holding a small plain black marble. Small, but surprisingly heavy. He needed both hands to carry it.

The Orc was transformed, almost handsome. He rubbed himself, "I feels grrrrreat! I don't itch no more. Amazin'", he looked down at Dominic, "Thank you, thank you so much."

Dominic smiled, he liked it when he made people happy. "Rub yourself all over with some green moss every morning and you'll stay this way. No more sores or warts."

"Come on you pasty no magic twerp, stop wasting time!" The goblin was hopping about with impatience.

Dominic showed the marble to Henry, "There, will that do?"

"I have no idea." Henry replied, "We are in completely uncharted territory here. I think the question is, 'are *you* happy with it?'"

Dominic nodded and put the marble in the recess, it looked small but made a solid clunk as he placed it. His headache was worse and he just wanted it, whatever it was going to be, to be over.

Henry raised his stick, "You will endeavour to seize your opponent's jewel and meld it with your own. Let the contest begin!" and as soon as his stick banged the ground, the goblin shot lightning out of both hands and Dominic was vaporised. He had the curious sensation of floating away from the cavern up towards a bright light.

Rising, rising, rising it was like being a conscious cloud but without the effort. He felt elated and peaceful. If this was death, then it wasn't so bad.

"Hello Dominic" said a familiar voice. Dominic twisted around to see his uncle. His uncle had passed away some years ago and Dominic reached out to hug him, but his arms clasped emptiness and passed through the apparition. His uncle smiled, "Sorry, but I'm not here physically. I have popped in with a message for you."

"What is it uncle?"

"I'm sorry but you have to go back Dominic, you have some very special tasks to do and you are the only one special enough to do them. It is your destiny Dominic."

"But uncle it's so peaceful here. Can't I stay?"

"Well, you have to earn the right to be here Dominic and it can be far from peaceful here just like down there. You must go back. I'll still be here when it is your time."

Dominic felt himself descending, down, down, down.

After blasting Dominic, the goblin looked around the obelisk and when he saw no-one there, launched into a frenetic victory jig. Kicking his legs and punching the air with his arms.

"Yeeeeessss! Yes, yes, yes, I knew it'd be easy-peasey. Stupid little boy, didn't know what he was doin'. Time to finish me jewel." The goblin snatched his big rock and then grabbed the marble, "Gaw it's heavy! It's going to make a real powerful jewel!" The goblin held them up over the white obelisk and pushed the two together. They merged, the black marble clearly in the centre of the big rock. The goblin pranced around uncontrollably full of himself.

"I win, I win, I win, I win, I win, I win…"

Henry banged his stick on the ground again "Alright, that's enough. You are free to go."

Cackling the goblin waved his prize at the crowd, "See! I'm free!" But it was then that the black marble burst and the whole rock turned black and goo started dribbling down the goblins arm. "Urgh, it tickles horrible!" A curious black glow surrounded the goblins hand with bright red and yellow sparks shooting off. "Owww! it's burnin', it hurts". The goblin tried to shake it loose but his hand wouldn't let go. "Oww, owwww. No! No! Oh! It's spreading, Argh! Argggghhh." the black glow surrounded the goblin, making him a prancing shadow of red and yellow sparks. Suddenly red flames shot out of the shadow in a burst of heat that made the front rows of creatures back away. With one final tortured scream the goblin vanished in a massive burst of flames and a rumble of thunder that made the cavern shake.

All the creatures stood looking at the empty platform. After several seconds had passed, they started looking at one another and then back at the platform. Finally, the Orc gave voice to what they were all thinking.

"Ain't there supposed to be one left?"

Henry walked over to the obelisk and then poked at the pile of ash that was the remains of the goblin. He was poking at it with his stick when the obelisk started to glow. To a hushed and awed crowd Dominic re-materialised on the platform.

"What happened to you?" asked Henry.

"I went somewhere and was told I had to come back." Dominic looked around. "The Goblin?"

"Turned to ashes" replied Henry

"What happens now?"

"The best advice I can give you is to firstly take your jewel and bond with it, then I suggest you return to the castle and tell Grand Wizard Tooks what has happened."

"But I don't have a jewel, remember?" Dominic was having trouble focussing, a fog clouded his brain and he hardly had the strength to stand.

Henry reached down into the pile of ash and extracted a large conical cut diamond, clear and bright. It sparkled and drew a gasp of awe from the crowd. "You do now" he replied. In a blur of limbs he spun a necklace of glittering silver silk with the jewel held in a mesh pouch. "There, touch it to the obelisk and then you are free to go."

When the diamond touched the obelisk Dominic's mind seemed to expand to encompass the whole universe. For an instant he was one with the cosmos, one with all the creatures in it, an integral part of the very essence of all creation, knowing and understanding everything. The next instant he was back in the cavern flat on his back with an even bigger headache than before.

"Ouch!"

"Come on young man," said Henry, helping him up, "I'll walk you back to the cavern, it's likely the dragon will need talking to."

They set off towards the tunnel. Dominic waved at the Orc on his way past and got a wave back. They walked to the tunnel in an emptiness of silence, every eye of the crowd quietly following them. They were about to enter when the first Orc from the tunnel lumbered up.

"Master, we's not sure but there may be an intruder come down the tunnel."

Henry bowed, "Thank you Grubbins, what makes you think there's an intruder?"

"Tingly feelings 'ere and there. Tunnel Tickler thought he felt a new outcrop of rock in the tunnel was warm, but no sighting of anyone."

Dominic looked down at the floor and kept his mouth shut.

"Well," said Henry, "Keep a sharp look out. Intruders can cause all sorts of chaos. We'll be careful."

"Yes Master." Grubbins returned to his post.

Henry led Dominic into the tunnel. The fireflies were there and danced around them in an aerial ballet lighting the way again.

"Ah, I see, natural light." said Henry, "Kept your magic signature at a minimum, clever. I'll remember that."

"What happened to the Goblin?" asked Dominic.

"Good question, I'm only guessing, as this has never happened before, but by creating a jewel out of the compressed badness from the Orc you made a sort of 'badness bomb'. When the Goblin merged it with its rock, it went off and poisoned the poor creature with a burst of concentrated nastiness. It didn't help that the goblins rock was of a substance that greatly amplifies the magic flowing through it. Our friend the goblin was a victim of its own greed."

Dominic forced tired legs to keep moving and blinked through his headache. Henry put out a hairy limb and helped Dominic along. Did some force of the universe prevent him from choosing a jewel so that he would have to make one on the spot? Or was it simply coincidence? His uncle's word's 'It is your destiny' circled around in his head. Well, to be accurate, the apparition of his uncle, it might not actually have been him. It was too much for his tired brain so he leant on the hairy arm and concentrated on keeping on walking.

In the cavern Grand Wizard Tooks and Professors Antimony and Glass were talking to the dragon. They all stopped and looked as Henry and Dominic entered.

"Henry!" said Grand Wizard Tooks.

"Cuthbert." replied Henry. "I'm returning one of your young proteges. He's successfully entered the underground caverns and completed the challenge of the opposites."

Grand Wizard Tooks looked down at Dominic in surprise, "Really, who helped him?"

"He did it all by himself as far as I can tell." Henry shrugged at the disbelieving faces of the three wizards, He walked over to them, "You are welcome to share my memories if you struggle with that."

They lent in close together, and little discharges of electricity passed between their heads. Dominic blinked, the cavern was starting to spin and he felt dizzy. He was saved from falling on his rear by the dragon who scooped him up in its wings. Enfolded in swathes of warm soft leather. Dominic curled up and felt secure. Voices drifted to him from far away.

"He's either the cleverest magician I've ever seen, or the luckiest. I'm not sure which one it is – maybe some of both?"

"We need to get some answers, now"

The dragons female voice "But the poor darling's exhausted, you must wait until tomorrow."

A short argument was terminated by a roaring and a bright orange glow.

"Tomorrow darlings, *TOMORROW!*...... The poor boy needs to sleep."

"Or else it's a trip to the burns unit for you three charming wizards. Is that clear enough for you?" said the mans voice

"Very well. You two will look out for him tonight?"

"Like he was my own egg, darling"

Dominic stoked the folds of soft leather, "Thank you." he whispered and fell asleep.

The End (for now!)

HERB GARDEN
by Joy S. Buchanan

Who are you? said the herb
Your scent wafts on the breeze
With long roots you can't kerb
You grow fast and with ease.

Said the plant, that is plain,
In a voice lush and calm,
Best for tea and tisane,
I'm the sweet lemon balm.

Another spoke up now
With its shoots slim and lithe,
To the wind I must bow
I'm the oniony chive.

And this lovely queen,
Yellow throng in her prime,
Variegated with green,
This array's golden thyme.

My leaves downy and strong
Are the crown of wise age,
My life span will be long
I'm the fine, hardy sage.

Spoke the one flat or curly
With strands growing sparsely
I'm a garnish, a garni
And proud to be parsley.

As a bush I unfold,
My life is no hassle,
Though I fade in the cold
In the warmth I am basil.

In the wind I must sway
By the star oleander –
Which is toxic, I say!
I am tart coriander.

Impatient, I can't wait,
In the sun's brilliant glint,
I will proliferate,
Call me mint, peppermint.

With my leaves evergreen
I'm the dew of the sea,
With my needles bright sheen,
I'm the mild rosemary.

Who thrives and is happy,
Summer fragrance each hour,
Constant friend to the bee,
I'm your lavender flower.

We live with each other
In the garden's clear air
Like sister like brother
With the jardinière.

End

THE THOUSAND-YEAR-OLD MAN
By Luke Carter

What comes to mind when you think of eternal life? If you'd have asked someone five-hundred years ago, you'd be declared a demon, imprisoned, and possibly exorcised. This wasn't actually as bad as it sounded if you played along. Two-hundred years ago, being declared a witch saw you burned alive or drowned. The latter was better, you could usually get out of the bonds and swim a bit down the river, as gross as it was, no-one could see you. Today, they'd probably laugh at you, call you insane or just claim you're writing a story about a new superhero. That's what makes today a lot easier than a lot of the past, people mostly just don't believe you because it's ridiculous. There are times I wish it were. What makes today the hardest, or at least for someone like me, not that there were others like me, is how connected and bureaucratic everything has gotten. Every country is connected to one another, and you can't get anywhere without increasingly harder to forge documents. I got tired of having to find a good forger, move somewhere and start a new life every decade or so, so I opted for the Ted Kaczinski method, you know, minus all the terrorism (I still kind of agree with a lot of what he suggested, society has become slaves to technology, but I might just be salty because of my own circumstances). For decades, I've lived in the rainforest, one of the last refuges for someone who doesn't want to be found. I arrived with nothing but a rucksack filled with clothes, hunting equipment, a tent, and few keepsakes I've held onto over the centuries as a reminder of where I come from. I started out just making a reasonable space for myself. Eventually I got tired of roughing it and built myself a log cabin. It took a while making all the raw materials I needed, but thankfully time was the something I had plenty of, that, water, and wood. Eventually I'd make myself a cot, a couple of chairs, a table, even incorporate a stone fireplace. I would hunt and forage whatever food I needed, and would use the bones, pelts, and spare wood to craft things. There're a few villages around that still obey the old bartering ways I grew up with. I'd sell my crafts if there was anything I needed that I couldn't make or just wanted the newspapers they'd occasionally get. After a decade or so I'd move my crafts to another village and do the same. I felt some people may have travelled from the previous villages but not enough to recognise me and a few that had, I claimed to be my own son and that seemed to get me the peace I wanted. And that was my life, until recently.

It's surprisingly quiet in the middle of the wilderness. Nature is loud, but when you get used to that, it's very easy to block out and when you get really used to it, three decades worth for instance, you can pick up subtle differences that can tell you a lot. Over the last few days I'd noticed a lot of wildlife migrating, travelling in one direction, much of it seeming distressed. I looked around a bit but couldn't find anything nearby. It was what woke me up the next morning that jarred me the most, the click from a DSLR camera, I knew it couldn't be anything good. I stepped out of my cabin, makeshift hatchet in hand, just in case. I walked around to the back of the cabin where stood, ear to the wall facing away from me, a woman holding said DSLR. I struck the cabin with the butt of my hatchet and she jolted around in surprise. She was beautiful and looked similarly aged as me, but I suppose that doesn't say very much, I stopped aging in my early 20s. There was also something eerily similar about her too, in an almost disarming sort of way.

"Desculpas, Bom Dia Amigo." She said, assuming I knew Portuguese, which I suppose was reasonable. Although I didn't exactly look Brazilian, I did know a bit of Portuguese, enough to barter and read the papers. I could also tell she wasn't a local, she was white, and her accent wasn't quite right.

"I was just checking if someone lived here. You do, I assume?" She continued in Portuguese.

"What do you want?" I responded sharply in Portuguese.

"Are you English?" She said in English.

"Yes." Although I hadn't been to England since the empire was thriving.

"Well, that's gonna make things a lot easier. I'm Cathy."

I simply nodded, not wanting to say too much. She continued "I'm just here taking pictures of the area and found your cabin. No-one is registered as living out here."

"Great, now you can leave." I went to go back inside.

"What about you?" I stopped and turned back.

"What about me?"

"Don't you know?"

"Know about what?" I was starting to get irritated.

"This whole area's being demolished. Thousands of square miles of rainforest. That's why I'm here, recording everything before it's all gone. And no offense, but it's the Brazilian government, they're not gonna care you live here, and I doubt your little axe is gonna do you much good."

I started looking around to see if I could see anything through the trees and brush. Nothing, but Cathy was being quiet and now I could hear, faintly in the distance, the forceful cracking of subsequent crashing of trees I the distance.

"How long do I have?"

"Hours, if you're lucky."

I ran into my cabin. I needed to leave, I didn't want to, but I suppose this was inevitable. Cathy came up to the door.

"Can I come in?" she asked gently. I looked at her for a second and figured it didn't matter at this point so nodded. "Is there anything I can do to help?"

"No. I need to leave." I snapped, it was a stressful situation to be in, one I hadn't planned for, but I won't make that mistake again. I needed to pack my things but my rucksack I'd just about worn out. I was down to using woven bags and baskets to carry my crafts to the villages. I'd need a tent; I'd cannibalised mine to help with the cabin. And my keepsakes, I'd have to decide.

"If you need to borrow my backpack, if that helps?" She was holding it out to me. She was actually quite sweet. "I only have a couple of lenses and some lunch anyway."

"Thank you." I appreciate the gesture so gave her one of my hand-woven bags for her stuff.

"Aww, thanks. Did you make this?"

"Yes." I said while wrapping my clothes around each keepsake and stuffing it in the bag, I was in such a rush, I accidentally knocked a candle stick holder I'd made from a mouse deer skull off the table which rolled under the cot. She looked around at the cabin, clearly not erected by experts. It was rough but it was home, for a time at least. *I'd need to get back to the village and figure out my next plan from there.* I thought to myself. *Maybe one of the other merchants at the village market could put me up.* She picked up the oldest keepsake of mine, an old toy my father had given me when I was a child, a bear carved from wood, aging horribly after a thousand years. She held it gently, analysing every detail of it as if it seemed familiar to her. I took it from her, wrapped and packed it. I grabbed a leopard skin cloak I'd made from a rival of mine a few years ago, he'd given me enough hassle. *Maybe now I could sell him for enough to get started.* I threw whatever crafts I could into the wicker basket and went to the exit.

"Okay, I'm ready to leave. I'll be in the village just north of here for a couple of days if you want your bag back." I said, ready to go. I was happy to just leave her here. She was just standing around, seemingly amazed by my soon-to-be-destroyed home.

"Hold on," she said kneeling down and reaching under the cot. I heard the subtle scraping of something small and metal against the wooden floor before she stood up with the skull candle stick holder. "What about this?"

"Keep it if you want."

"I also found… this." She held up an old gold coin. Dammit it, how could I have forgotten that. "Is… is this a solidus?"

"What do you know about them?"

"Only that they're from, like, the early Ottoman Empire and… extremely rare." She kept pausing between words. She then looked around again. "I tell you what, I wouldn't usually do this, but if you let me take some pictures of your cabin, you can stay with me until you figure out what you need to do."

"Why would you do that?"

"Because I think we might have something in common."

Cathy and I walked into a cabin she had rented in one of the villages I traded from. She set her stuff down by the slept-in of the two beds. I was about to walk in when she blocked my path, getting up close and personal.

"What are you doing?" I asked, confused.

"I wanna know one more thing about you."

"We've just spent the last two hours walking and talking." I responded indignantly.

"No, I spent the last two hours talking about me. You spent that time grunting and avoiding questions."

"Then what do you want to know."

"Your name."

I started into her unwavering eyes, trying to avoid scowling at her else she wouldn't believe whatever I said.

"Julian." I said matter-of-factly.

"Okay, now your real name." She said, seeing through my lie.

It took me by surprise, I wasn't expecting her to call me out, but I decided lying wasn't the way here. I could've just found another place to stay but I still needed to know what she meant by having something in common. I couldn't just leave, so I had to know what she really wanted. "What does it matter?"

"I need to be able to trust you. But how can I trust a man who lies to me about his name."

"You've only just met me, you don't know anything about me. To trust someone you've only just met is foolish." I spoke from the point of view of experience, and in my experience, trusting people had only ever caused me trouble or hurt, in one form or another. She stepped away from me and the door, wandering about the room as she talked, I stayed at the doorway out of respect.

"That might've been the case once, but the world has changed from when that was an absolute rule. And I think you'll find I know a lot more about you than you think. I know you use the name Julian because it's a name you can use to blend it easily. I know you're much older than you look." That statement worried me. Did she know my secret? She didn't have enough evidence and that was a big leap. She continued. "I know you're well travelled, even been to Constantinople." She tossed me the solidus. I caught it and checked my pocket thinking she'd picked it, but no, mine was right there. I pulled it out and compared the two. Identical!

"How--?"

"Do you remember how you got yours?" She asked. I thought back to a hundred years prior. I was in France. I'd met a woman, an archaeologist. Deep black hair, pale skin, glasses, wearing the French fashion of the time. I'd been a soldier at Versailles and elected to stay in France for a while. We grew close and spent the night together. In my vulnerability, I'd confessed to always having wanted a keepsake of Constantinople from before its fall in the 1400s. I had to cover myself by saying the time-period fascinated me or else I wasn't making sense. The next morning she was gone, but the solidus had been left on her pillow.

I looked at Cathy who stopped and looked back at me with a familiar caring looking I hadn't seen since that night.

"I had my suspicions back then, but I wasn't sure." She said so softly, it almost sounded like an apology.

I was stunned still, unable to do anything other than stare between her and the coins in my hand.

She asked me again, "What's your name?"

Back then I'd used my real name again, and somehow, she knew.

"Gregory Stourbridge."

She smiled a beautiful smile that brought me a sense of peace. It'd been so long since I'd felt that.

"I think it's time you met the others." She said as though I was just meant to make sense of it.

"Others?!"

"Yes, others like us. A collective sworn to keep an accurate historical record of our world. And they'll want to meet you."

I followed Cathy halfway around the world for a few weeks before she took me to this collective. Cathy was well covered with her forged documents, however we had to make due to a few concessions on our journey as I had nothing, smuggling ourselves aboard cargo ships and freight trains. We caught up on the last 100 years. She told me she was not long past 500 years old but was only recruited by the collective shortly before she'd met me, because she was still very new to the idea of others like us, she didn't want to risk exposing herself. She updated me about the world and how it'd moved so fast. In many ways it was unrecognizable to the world I'd left behind, but in far too many ways, it was no different or so much worse.

We arrived at what I supposed they would call a headquarters though Cathy hadn't given me an actual name for it. It was a smaller building than I'd been expecting, a townhouse in the centre of London in an area I'm sure, once upon a time, I might've known well. We walked in and it was easily the cleanest environment I'd been in for a long time. The walls had a fascinating blend of Victorian architecture yet modern designs throughout. Under a set of stairs, a door led to further stairs that took us below the house. At the bottom of the stairs, hallways branched out in all directions as far as the eye could see, stretching under and throughout the borough. I was in awe of what was around me. These buildings had been here for so long I remember them being built yet I had no idea all of this being built beneath.

Cathy directed me through the maze of corridors for what felt like a mile until we reached the end of one hallway and to an old-fashioned solid wood door labelled 'The Consult'. Cathy checked the time before we entered.

"We're a couple of minutes early." She told me, pleased with herself. "We'll just wait."

When the time was up, I followed Cathy into the room. It was huge. It looked like a court room, stands for seating around the edge of the room reminded me of the Houses of Parliament. There were a lot of people sat along them, staring at me like I was a relic in a museum. Most of them looked young, barely out of their twenties or thirties. I wasn't used to this sort of attention; it made me uncomfortable. At the end of the room, I saw five people sat at a long, old wooden desk; they were of various races, three were old, the other two were about my age, or at least my appearance.

I stepped into the court facing the people on the bench like a deer in headlights, well out of my depth. A woman, sat in the middle chair, stood up; clearly the oldest of the group.

"We would like the welcome you, Gregory. We have anticipated your arrival since Cathy alerted us to your presence." She said regally. Her accent was undeterminable, she spoke the kings English, but I could hear the centuries of adapting to colloquial times in her voice. "My name was formerly Wassa, I am now known as Mabel. As a fellow elder, you reserve the right to address any of us elders by our birth names." She points to the man and woman to the right of her. "Here we have Lucian and Amanda." Then she gestures to the man and woman to her left. "And here are Edric and Elena. I hope you'll get to know us all on more personal level and choose how you wish to address us."

She sat back in her seat. I stood there, watching this ceremony, glancing around at the crowd muttering around me. I could see many uniforms of all types, different professional dress wear indicating these people were spread out, living normal lives. I looked back to Mabel.

"If you have chosen to reject your birth names then I request to be referred to as Julian." I declared.

"I don't see that being a problem." Mabel said looking at her fellow Elders.

"You have mentioned elders, please elaborate. Aren't we all ancient here?" I enquired.

Edric, the only man sat amongst the elders of colour and appearing similar to my age, formally raised his hand while turning to the elders, and Mabel nodded.

"As you may have noticed, you have aged." Has stated. I nodded in agreement. "Despite appearances, we are not immortal or eternal. Our aging has slowed down significantly, about 100 years to one. We will all die. Unfortunately for many of our kind, it is not easy to reach an age such as yours or ours. Many are often found out, or simply fall victim to violence or accidents. Mabel here sits as our Eldest at 6,000 years. She is the only second generation elder on this council. The rest of us are third or fourth."

"Edric. If I may, that's an Anglo-saxon name, correct?" I asked, he nodded. "Is that a birth name, or adopted?"

"I chose this name. I was born in Kenya as Mafi but captured as a slave in the early 1700s. After arriving in Wales, I was given a slave name. I was found, eventually, by members of this council and freed. That is when I chose this name." Edric answered.

"I am sorry for your hardship." I said directly to him before addressing the rest of the council. "But this means you are fully aware of the atrocities of man." The Elders all leant forward in their chairs. "I know something of awful working conditions myself. The history of suffering many of the working class and minorities have had to suffer through the centuries. I have seen it, and I have suffered it, as have far too many other people."

Cathy stared at me, concerned, but I had to ignore it. Something had gotten to me about all of this, and I had to let it out.

"So much of the pain I have seen has been caused by people in power, either through action, or inaction. And you sit up there on your podium of pride exclaiming yourself elders, yet I see no responsibility taken from any of you, and it's the people that have suffered." I'd finished, yet it felt like I had so much more to say, but I knew I'd said what was needed. I turned around and left the room. Cathy looked back between me and the elders in bewilderment before chasing after me.

After I'd left the room, I reached a crossroad in the corridor and wasn't sure which way to go. Cathy came through the door and caught up to me.

"What the hell was that?" She exclaimed.

"I thought I'd made myself pretty clear in there." I said, looking down the corridors, trying to figure out which way to go, avoiding looking Cathy in the eye.

"Why would you let me bring you here if all you were planning to do was tell them where to shove it?"

I finally looked at her so she could see the truth of what I had to say in my eyes.

"Because I didn't know until I got here. I saw all this spectacle. This didn't just happen. It took effort, planning, and immeasurable resources. Something they—" I had to stop myself for a moment and compose myself before

110

continuing. "Something the world needs, and they've sat back and let everything wrong in the world happen."

She looked at me for a moment, seeing something was below the surface. She looked behind her and the door started to open. She grabbed my arm and lead me down the corridor to the left.

"Come with me."

We navigated the labyrinth of corridors for about 5 minutes, barely saying a word to one another. We reached a room, Cathy pressed her bracelet against the handle and it open.

As we walked into the room, the lights came on automatically reveal a quaint studio apartment. Walls covered in memorabilia of the last century, newspaper clippings, pictures, and drawings. At the end of the room was a large window somehow displaying a penthouse view of the city. I pointed to it.

"How—"

"Oh." She looked at the window, walked over to it and pressed a button below the windowsill. The screen turned off. "Guess you're not used to HD yet. Welcome to my home, this is where I've been living for the last 70 years or so."

"Why'd you bring me here?"

She went over to a shelf filled with tatty notebooks. She pulled one out near the end of the shelf, opened it towards the middle, then passed it over to me.

"These are my first drafts I submit to the archive." I read through the pages of handwritten notes. This segment was from the 19th century about the deaths of indigenous children in Canada with detailed drawings of mass-grave sites. I had to admit it was hard to take in. I eventually got to a bit that described a man called Reggie who tried to stop the massacre and ended up in the grave too.

"You've gone into a lot of detail about this man, Reggie. Who is he?" I could see she was already uncomfortable before I asked the question.

"He... He was my husband. I'd met him through The Collective." She spoke so softly. All these years later it was clearly still difficult to talk about. "He tried to stop the deaths of these children who didn't deserve the fate the colonists decided for them. They killed him for speaking against god's wishes to convert these children and 'save their souls' and I was powerless to do anything about it. So I recorded it."

"I'm sorry, I had no idea—"

"Of course you didn't. But the truth is, there have been attempts to change the future and it never ended well. We've lost elders to this. I can't imagine what you've been through over the years, and all alone, it must've been unbearable. But don't for a second think any less of us because we couldn't change what we wanted."

"Grant me the serenity to accept the things I cannot change, courage to change the things I can, and wisdom to know the difference." I quoted. Cathy cracked a sweet smile that lit up the room.

"That was one of Mabel's, actually." She chuckled. I was dumfounded. "But now, we are in an era of history we have been waiting so patiently for. Because of my records, we were able to incorporate this accurate history into curriculums and sources for academics which led to the discovery of these children all these years later. That is why we keep the records, in hopes that they will eventually see the light of day." These people clearly had had an influence on the world around them, even if not as explicit as I had hoped.

"My father was a gong farmer for a castle where I grew up. I couldn't even tell you where that is now." I confessed to her. "He was shunned by everybody around him because of his profession, and his smell. He grew bitter and drunk. And he was a mean and terrible drunk. My mother always claimed God would seek his salvation, but I didn't want his salvation. Eventually a war came, and my father was conscripted. He died fighting, but not one man mourned for him. Before I met you, I'd fought in The War, I'd lost friends and I couldn't figure out why we had to die. To me it made no sense. I couldn't justify it, so when war came again, I ran to the 'States. Then I saw how people were treated for something out of their control, race, gender, sexuality. Something I found so trivial in my many years, they used as a dividing point to crack the population into pieces. Then came more war, more hate. I'd had enough. That why I disappeared." I didn't even realise but we were holding hands.

"Since my husband died, I'd really struggled to find someone I could connect to," she told me. "But I met you and, I dunno, I felt like I was almost talking to him again. I wasn't sure about you, I didn't know if we could live a life together, and the idea of losing someone again scared me. That's why I ran away. I'd kind of hoped the solidus I left for you might lead you back to me if my suspicions about you were correct. I'm glad it did."

Staring into one another's eyes, our grips tightening, we both closed our eyes and leant towards each other. We spent the night in each other's embrace, getting to know each other like that night in France all those decades ago, but this time, with nothing to hide.

The next morning, I called another meeting of the Elders. There weren't nearly as many people in attendance, but all five elders came. I walked up to the centre of the court again, Cathy stood behind me.

"Elders, I wish to convey a sincere apology for my actions yesterday. They were unfair accusations and based on ignorance. I pray you're willing to forgive me." I pled. There was a moment of silence as they considered what I'd said before Mabel stood up and addressed me.

"So Julian, you confess you were wrong?"

"No," I said directly. Mabel sat back down. "I believe in what I said. I just understand more now of what you do here and its importance. What I said was correct, but I was disrespectful in how I said it and for that, I apologise. You play a very long game and are only just now reaping the benefits of the work The Collective has done. But I stand by my call for a more active approach."

They took a moment before conferring amongst themselves. Edric stood.

"We have strict protocols here designed to ensure we are not discovered. We tread a fine line and risk much to do what we do now. You have been withdrawn for society a long time and in that time the world has changed significantly. It is connected more now than ever before. Every time one of us steps out in public, they risk their picture being posted online which further risks our people being discovered years from now. A more active approach would only endanger us more." Edric said caringly before sitting back down. He wasn't trying to assert dominance or order me around; he was a man looking out for his people as they all were.

"I beg you, please hear what I have to say and consider—" I said before was cut off by Lucian.

"Enough. You have disrespected this council, you have no understanding of the extent of our operation, you come in here demanding a change of operation. I don't know who you think you are but it will not stand." Lucian condemned. There was a lull in the room as I thought of what to say but before I figured it out, Cathy came to my rescue. She walked up beside me and addressed the council.

"Members of the council. What Julian has to say is worth hearing." She pleaded. "He speaks from a lifetime of experiences, dozens in fact, he only wants to do what's right."

Mabel stood to respond. "Cathy, while you are not on this council, your connection to it cannot be denied. On that dark day, you lost a husband, and we lost a colleague." That's when it dawned on me, Reggie wasn't just another member, he was an elder. "You of all people must understand why we cannot interfere but merely observe and record."

Cathy acquiesced.

"She does understand, more than I can possibly imagine, but what Reggie did was right, and proved himself an honourable man by doing so. And what his actions showed was a desire by this council to do what is right, not simply observe and witness. We have the power to effect real change. Many who seek power only see life in terms of their lifespan, however we have the benefit of our foresight being directly informed by our hindsight. We

115

are not victims of false information or manipulation from figureheads and mass-media. We have the ability to look back at what history was truly like, why it was the way it was, and effect the change necessary. I understand the risk of being in the public eye, but I am not suggesting we take over the positions of power, but instead position ourselves to influence power. You already have people in influential positions, else all of this wouldn't be here. And I would assume you have similar set ups around the world, and if not, we can. If there's one thing we have, it's time. We can make good change to this world."

The Elders spoke amongst themselves for a moment before informing us they would need to confer privately reach their verdict. They left via a door behind them.

Cathy came close to me and held my hand, squeezing it.

"I really hope they're willing to listen." She hoped.

We waited around for a while before hearing the door open and a mix of both anticipation and dread filled both of us. Cathy's hand squeezed mine so hard I felt like it might break. They all took their seats apart from Mabel who remained standing. They had no tells, I couldn't figure out what was on their minds.

"We have debated your proposal." She started, giving nothing away. "Out of fairness to you, we weighed the options and wished to look at things objectively. We considered your plea, it's merits and its potential risks. While it can be said we have been complacent, the concern of risk to this organisation as well as its occupants, the protection of which has always been the priority of this council." She paused for a moment, looking back to her follow elders. That second felt longer than a dozen lifetimes. She turned back to us. "After great discussion and a majority rule, we have decided that your proposal is not only reasonable, but also a moral imperative."

I was so elated I didn't know what to do, what to say. Cathy jumped at me with joy, hugged me so tight I could've popped.

"Thank you, council," I said, the only thing that seemed right. "You won't regret this."

We spent months devising a plan, and longer implementing it. New divisions were set up for all manner of problem solving but it didn't matter how long it took.

#

I placed a full stop on the page in a thick, leather-bound book. I was sitting at a solid wood desk positioned by a window with a view of the countryside and rolling green hills. I remember Cathy walked up behind me, as though she knew. She wrapped her arms around my shoulders in a loving embrace, placed her chin on my shoulder and spoke softly in my ear.

"Finally finished?" She asked.

"Finally? I didn't realize I was on a deadline." I said jovially.

"What's next?"

"Well, we still need to sort the mess that is Congress, there's the trafficking rings in Asia, Africa, and Europe we need to find connections for, not to mention getting food to those throughout Europe. At this point, I'm starting to feel like a thirty-year vacation wasn't enough."

"Not that, you old fool." Cathy said. She pulled over a chair and sat down so I turned to face her. "You know only those within the collective will get the chance to read this?"

"Of course," I said reassuringly. I took her hands and looked deep into her eyes, talking from the heart. "Those who join the collective deserve to know why we changed things. They deserve to know who we are, who we once were, and why the work we do is so important. And hopefully, when we are long gone, they will heed our lessons and make them their own."

I turned back to my desk, looked out the window once more as if to say *'it's time'* and closed the book. Written on the front, engraved in the leather, was its title: "Tales of The Thousand-Year-Old Man by Gregory Stourbridge."

End

THE WORLD OF TAZ
by Joy S. Buchanan

Taz, wanderer over soft silk sands

Ruffled by the sea,

With hands of gold on silver bands

Threads gems for you and me.

On beaches bathed in burning light

Gorgeous in the sun

Taz travels with his jewels bright

Admired by everyone.

With gentle hands and twinkling eye

Quickly as can be

He spreads his cargo 'neath the sky

A blaze of jewellery.

Now twinkles bright the eye that sees

Arrayed reflected light

Those timeless diadems that please

And satisfy the sight.

For you and me Taz fashions free

Necklaces and rings

A fantasy all glittery

A treasury of things.

He has no time to linger here

Or to rest awhile

His wares all strewn soon disappear

All ordered is the pile.

And Taz goes onwards on his quest

Wandering amain

O'er soft silk sands by foaming crest

Till he returns again.

End

DEAD OR ALIVE?
By Rowland Cook

"GET OUT OF MY OFFICE!" the short middle-aged detective bristled with indignation. However, the younger man opposite was not fazed by the venom dripping from the demand.

"Now then, Detective Bream, that's not very nice."

"I do not believe in being nice to murdering scum. Just because you got away with it doesn't give you the right to come here and gloat. Now fuck off before I lose control and smash your smug sanctimonious face in!"

The urbane and handsome object of Bream's ire casually reached into his pocket and produced a small digital recorder. "As you wish, but before I go just listen to this phone call I recorded. It only lasts a minute."

Bream sat, a picture of pure solid hatred as the young man placed the recorder on his desk and clicked the playback button. There was the sound of ringing followed by the telephone connecting and then a sinister voice spoke quietly,"You sold me a fake, the girl didn't die."

There was a long pause, then the young man's voice replied, "I assure you it was a genuine snuff movie, that was just the defence we used in court."

The quiet voice went on, "Prove it, or else I will come for you."

"What? You want me to take you to where she is buried and dig her up?"

"That would do."

Another long pause, and then the young man's voice came again. "You will come in person, alone, to the coordinates I will give you. Ring again in a couple of days. I have to work out which one she was."

The young man clicked off the recorder and put it back in his pocket. "My defence in court was that I used special effects to fake the death of the actress and that is the truth. I know you don't believe it, but I had reasons not discussed in court that I will explain to you. I will introduce you to the actress and you can talk to her. I have led this man on so you trap the monster who bought the movie. It seems the least I can do for what you went through in court. But if you want me to go I will." and he got up and made for the door.

Bream's face twitched as bitter memories of his humiliation in court lacerated his mind like shrapnel. The young man was opening the door. "Wait!" Bream's agonised face lapsed into resignation as the young man came back and sat down.

#

Three hours later they were in a private hospital looking down on a pretty girl who was in a coma. The young man was visibly upset, "You see, Maddy was going to be my wife and the star of my movie. But her brakes failed and she had a nearly fatal car crash. She has been in a coma ever since. She did not have medical insurance and we had to find a lot of money very quickly. "

Bream looked at him, "The snuff movie was for her medical care?"

"Yes, a friend of a friend of someone sinister had approached us previously. They offered us a huge sum. With special effects being so good, we thought we could make the movie without actually doing anyone harm."

Bream did not look convinced. The young man beckoned to the door and a girl entered wearing a silver wig and a black catsuit. The young man gestured at her, "Here is your victim Detective, Maddy's best friend Claire. She is a special effects specialist and, as you can see, she is very much alive."

Bream had not been convinced by the procession of similarly attired actresses that had been paraded into court during the defence. But he had to admit he was convinced by Claire.

#

Two days later, as the sun rose over the desert, a convertible wound a dusty trail to the pre-arranged spot. The young man got out and waited with a shovel, listening to the chirping of the cicadas. Before long a large black pickup truck arrived and a tall balding man got out wearing a black suit.

"OK, show me." Same quiet voice as on the phone. The young man dug down a few feet and then his shovel hit wood. Moments later a coffin sized box was opened to reveal the body, still dressed in a black catsuit and silver wig. The young man gestured, "Satisfied?".

The black suit drew a gun and flashed a badge, "FBI! You are under arrest. In fact, I have a good mind to shoot you right now, so don't try anything."

A helicopter buzzed in fast with the word 'POLICE' on its side in big white letters. It's loudspeaker barked "Police! Drop the gun."

The young man ducked down into the shallow grave as the FBI waved his badge and shouted "FBI" again. All to no avail over the roaring of the helicopter's engines and the clattering of its blades. There was the crack of a rifle and a puff of dust at the agent's feet. Cursing he got down on the ground and looked angrily at the young man peeking over the lip of the grave.

As the helicopter landed, three more black pickups arrived and a bunch of police and FBI agents spent some time pointing pistols and shouting at each other. It had been a sting operation. Once everyone had calmed down, two angry and frustrated bunches of lawmen had to admit the body was a life-like shop window mannequin.

"I did this for the scene where I dump the body." the young man explained. They had no choice but to let him go.

#

The next day the young man sat in the park with Claire in a secluded spot away from prying eyes. She looked puzzled,

"So where did you hide the body? I tracked your cell phone to the same spot as before."

The young man looked around before he replied, "It's under the fake grave, a few feet further down. I figured no one would carry on digging once they found the box and, thankfully, I was right."

"I bet they were pretty put out?"

"That's putting it mildly. I can't believe you talked me into burying her. I know we needed the money but I can't get her screaming out of my mind. I feel unclean on the inside and nothing I do relieves the pain."

"Don't you get any ideas of telling!" Claire's voice took on a hard edge, "You were the one who produced it. You were the one who covered it up and you were the one who buried the body. It will all come back to you and you know it. It will be the death sentence for you if you confess."

"And you," said the young man, "I've got the whole thing on video tape, you didn't know it but you left fingerprints, I took copies of the full video and I have voice recordings that implicate you in it too. So don't you get any ideas either."

"Ohhhhh!" Claire frowned, "That's nasty!"

The young man's head snapped around to look at her, "I'll tell you what's nasty, murdering your twin sister, that's nasty! You ruined everything for me tampering with the special effects and blowing her chest wide open for real. No one is interested in me as a director now, nor can I get anyone to act in my own projects."

Claire's face hardened, "Bitch had it coming, she tormented me from the very first day we were born. She screwed the brakes on Maddy's car to take her out so she'd get the part in your next movie."

"You don't know that." The young man couldn't keep the bitterness from his voice. They froze as an elderly couple creaked by in slow motion. Once the couple had shuffled out of earshot, Claire put her hand on his knee.

"She's done it before, she was always hanging out with my father at his garage. Pops kept mum's Mustang running perfect. Then, just after mum forbade Sis to go to acting school, its brakes failed and mum was killed. My father died of a broken heart six months later thinking he'd messed up the servicing. Sis was a monster!"

The young man picked up her hand and put it gently back in her lap, "I'm finished here, I'm going back to Europe to try and start over. If Maddy wakes up, give me a call. Goodbye."

"Whatever!" muttered Claire quietly as he walked away.

End

TRYING TO KILL MARCONI
by Martin Hilyard

I stepped out of the portal, tired, dirty and defeated. The technicians were still there, as ugly as ever. Their sour faces turned away and they moved indifferently towards the next upcoming. Instead of heading home I paused to wait for the new arrival, though God knows I needed sleep.

The famous blue haze shimmered briefly, there was that thunderous crack of air being displaced and the slight smell of sulphur that no-one could quite explain. Another agent had made it back. It was Kemminger, a trickle of blood marking a handsome black face made grey with fatigue. I watched as the technicians helped him out of his protective gear, moving carefully as if he were made of glass or might pop out of existence at a wayward touch. All the time he stared impassively at me, his dark eyes drooping with fatigue.

Once released, I nodded and fell into step as he shuffled towards the exit. There was no debriefing necessary, nothing to wait for. If we came back we had failed. Only if we ceased to exist would we know we had succeeded. The paradox had long since lost its fascination; only oblivion beckoned.

"How'd it go ?" I asked, knowing already.

He carried on walking as I waited for an answer. Four hundred years is a long way to come back from. Finally he managed to speak.

"The usual. The grandfather assignment. I tried introducing a virulent carcinoma, something to permanently cripple the gene structure. Breakfast. In his mush, the old heathen. He ate it up and asked for more."

Bitterness etched every word, and a hatred as malignant as any cancer. I knew how he felt.

"I was so angry I tried knifing the bastard. Fell off the stoop and cut my face. The Inertia Effect."

Yeah, the Inertia Effect. Two things kept us from completing our mission. The Paradox of Continuity and the Inertia Effect. Murder was not as easy as it looked.

I grunted something and he lapsed into a moody silence. Looking ahead, I almost cried out. We were coming up to The Window. I shuddered, not wanting to look but drawn to it as always. Light flickered through the polarised glass, waiting for someone to pass. In that corridor the shadows we cast were born by the fires of a dying earth.

Kemminger stopped as well but moved away and crossed his arms. Isolation was our only defence against despair. War raged across the city. In the hills light blossomed. Here and there were great ravening fires. Towers fell. Above the shielding domes, the plasma mines of the Shussharin hovered, our final defence against the dark ships of the Enemy, the Dromon.

As I watched the light flickered and I saw the split-second flash of an energy gun. The thin scream of the dying could faintly be heard as Time began to infect Berkeley. The old human buildings vanished and a squalid tenement of worker burrows erupted like toadstools, fixated and became solid, eternal. We were losing the war.

We watched for a while. Finally two, no three humans managed to fight their way out. One fell and had

128

to be dragged away, a woman I think. The Dromen, the low-class runts of Dromon society fired after them with primitive energy weapons, then slouched back into the burrows, fighting amongst themselves to get in. Across the whole planet it was the same. The last men, fighting for a planet that did not exist, in the hope of saving one that had already died.

I gazed at the polluted city. Were there more Dromon domes? Had the plague spread? I looked for landmarks and saw with dismay that the Bay Bridge had gone. The Dromon used no ground vehicles of course. What looked like a smart suburb of domes and solar gardens was beginning to infect the Bay Area. Even so, fires blossomed as we fought back.

"Bloody lizards," Kemminger muttered and began to walk away. He moved like an old man and it didn't take me long to catch up.

"They're not," I said, correcting him. "More like land crocodiles. We think their planet dried up and they had to evolve."

He stopped abruptly, his face like a tired panther's, worn and trapped.

"That's what we become," he snarled. "That's what you'll become, you fucking cretin!"

I stopped and let him walk away. He was right, of course.

After that it took me a while to get to my dome. Everything nowadays worked by genetic verification: doors, gates, travelways and portals, everything. It took time for the poor scanners our remaining electronics industry could turn out to analyse stuff like that. And the streets were dangerous, you had to take care. When any human could transform into a Droman at any time, you did your best to keep things out or the killers in. Once home I left all my weapons in the safebox and headed for my cell. Exhausted, I took no food and barely had time to snap on the cuffs before I fell into an uneasy sleep.

When the moon rises, I will go to the high plateau and take my ease.

I awoke, eyes gummed, my mouth foul. I tried to rise but stopped, defeated. Drained already, I fumbled a hand across the ident tab and the cuffs fell away. Sitting on the side of the bed I stared wearily at the metal restraints and wondered what I would do if they ever failed to open. This was who we had become. The only measure of sanity left was that a man remembered to restrain himself.

People had changed in the night of course, transformed, become that which we most dread, a Droman. It was something primeval in us, that fear. The usurpation of human stock, the inflow of the alien. Maybe we carried the fear of the neanderthal even now, conscious perhaps that those old, old faces walked the same streets.

Today was another assignment day and the latecall was already singing stridently in the next room. Everybody was in the military these days and the generals made sure you reported. Every dome was keyed to their local army monitor station. Cosy.

I dressed lethargically, my mind sluggish, already thinking about the day's work. I was beginning to doubt that we could do it, despite what our allies, the Shussharin said or pulsated or whatever they did. Being energy lattices I, like many others, assumed they used telepathy and that made my skin crawl. Only the generals and leaders had ever seen them and what they had seen they didn't say. Whatever it was had made the hardest of them look old and grey, defeated already. That was enough for me.

I collected my weapons and headed for the walkie. The elevator door opened and three men emerged, struggling with a fourth. I stepped back. Another one! I gazed at the prisoner, saw with revulsion the slight build, the stooping shoulders, his stained fingers. Anger surged and I stepped forward and hit him a stinging blow across the face.

His captors looked surprised. One protested, "Hey, fella, no need for that," then they hustled the marconi on. I just stood there, watching the elevator door open and close impotently, my hand hurting from the blow.

All over earth, the marconis were appearing. The Shussharin were baffled, it was said, nothing like it had happened before. It was as if some different laws of physics applied to this part of the universe. People changed. They became secretive, reclusive. They stole equipment, cables, began experiments. Eventually they were caught, hopefully before they had managed to send out a signal. The Shussharin said we had to stop them or the Dromon would go on finding us and everything would be in vain.

But they were people and if we ever succeeded in putting Time right, they would change back. So we didn't kill them, the way we killed the Dromen, but imprisoned them, far from anything to do with radio, where they couldn't hurt us any more.

The scientists said it was because of the strange warping of time and space in this part of the galaxy that had led Einstein up the garden path and made him just another footnote. But my grandparents were neochristians and something from their past was in my bones. I thought we wanted to die. When part of a race defied every known law to summon creatures that would hunt them down, every one, those beings wanted to die. Even a fool like me knew that. But only a wise man would know why.

I will stand in the Light of Giving. I will sleep the one-lid sleep. I will go down into the dust and wisdom will come.

When I got to the Project there was good news. The engineers had managed to locate a segment of time when Marconi could be reached without danger. When we realised what had happened and the Shusharrin told us what to do, everyone thought it would be easy. Go back four hundreds years or so and kill the son of a bitch, no matter what effect it had on us. But violence didn't seem to work. Assassins had been sent back with all manner of weapons, poisons, energetics, projectiles, even bludgeons. Nothing worked. The moment the agent returned to now-time, something reasserted itself.

Marconi spent his life feeling slightly queasy, had headaches and stumbled often but didn't die. I have even seen videos of the moment, split seconds before he finally sent the signal, when an atomic bomb arrived, set to explode. Only it didn't.

So now we were trying a different tack. Don't try to stop him, change him, change something else. Agents roamed time trying to kill physicists and financiers, bombed metal shops that had provided components, thinkers who had provided inspiration. I even heard they tracked down Copernicus and killed him to see what would happen. No good. But they're still trying.

132

Marconi had got nowhere in Italy, his home country. People had just ignored him. So there was a group trying to get him to forget about radio. It was kind of interesting. Go back with something that would make him famous and successful. Persuade people to back him. He'd never pursue the crazy idea of sending messages without wires, never send the signal that had brought the Dromon from four hundred light years away to destroy mankind.

That's what gave me nightmares, thinking about it. Marconi's signals had propagated in all directions at the speed of light. They'd taken four hundred years to reach the Dromon sphere, arriving in 2302 AD. Paranoid, warlike, barbarous, the Dromon constantly monitored space for modulated signals as the first indication of an intelligent species that might threaten them.

By using Dirac, that strange, paradoxical warping that allowed them to travel to the exact point in space - and time - that a signal emanated from, they had arrived above Italy moments after his successful experiment had ended. From that moment on, war on Earth had been incessant. But not our Earth. We remembered four hundred years of history that had never happened. I had never happened.

What it was, the Shussharin explained, was that time wasn't linear but a spiral with many branchings. From any point of change, it took time for that moment to catch up with and overtake history. The first indications of the change were the Dromon appearances. A great wave of non-being was sweeping from the past into our present. Eventually it would arrive and wipe us out, except for the few hundred thousand real Earth people they had managed to evacuate to other planets before the Dromon sterilised the world.

The Shussharin wouldn't say when it would arrive. I wondered why we kept trying. After all, the human race had been saved for now, safe on some secret planet light years away. So why did we bother? I pondered that for a while. It wasn't to be heroes, I know that. Heroes aren't dirty and tired and full of hate. Deep down I believe none of us fear death. But change terrifies us, especially change that comes from outside, that alters and corrupts. Sometimes it's like rape, a forceful irruption in our lives. Sometimes it's the black, choking realisation that overnight our once-bright soul has the canker-black shell of a cockroach. That's what I was fighting.

When the blue sun rises and my blood sings then, like war and anguish, I will take her.

I prepared for my mission, the blood gravid in my veins, a dull grating in my ears. Some sadist had piped pictures from The Window into the portal monitor so I could watch the city being pulverised. The glow of Dromon energetics splashed against the domes, lurid and alive.

I turned away, a volcanic anger growing inside me. As the portal operated I turned back, in time to see a greenish tinge cover the technicians, a stutter in space like paper tearing. Then the back of my head was introverted and flung through parts of my body I had problems holding onto. I screamed.

Blue sky poured down on me, a torrent of heat that drove the chill from my blood and made me light-headed. Italy, 1894. I looked around, caught sight of the two gypsy caravans where the team was located and strolled over. Their mission was a little different to mine. Since nothing seemed to stop Marconi sending the signal, why not jam it, make it seem like normal interstellar noise?

134

They were ready, waiting. At the exact moment Marconi pulled his switch, we would pull ours. My job wasn't to make sure the experiment didn't work. My job was to make sure Marconi got the message it would never work.

I clambered the steps of the nearest caravan and opened the door. The walls and ceiling were crammed with equipment, lights blinking irregularly. The technicians were still, absorbed, grime around their collars. They didn't look up so I slammed the door and jumped back down again.

It took a while to walk to the Marconi house but I didn't hurry. I had plenty of time. The air was still, deadly still, but I could feel something massive moving, pressing down. I reached the house and sat down on a nearby bench. No-one knew what would happen if the signal was jammed, it had never been done before. I suppose he'd come out, walk across the street as he had done a dozen times before. Only this time I'd be waiting.

I closed my eyes and the blood began to sing in my veins. I could feel myself swelling, a sense of pregnant expectation. Like victory, not yet won but certain. My skin felt dry, like parchment. I heard the door slam, the cursing undertone he always used, and opened my eyes. I saw his hated face again, the shifting eyes and harassed expression. I stood, forgetting my mission, reached for the concealed weapon. He stopped, looked around, then skyward. His mouth flew open as a shadow occulted the sun and I fired into his back, a surge of animal pleasure thrilling me.

He pitched forward, blood and bone flying, and slumped onto the red Umbrian earth. There was no surprise in his death, only the manner of his dying, as though I had never seen it happen before. Then the recall tripped and I was grabbed, turned inside out and flattened, the realisation that I had done it resonating out into Space.

I arrived back, exhausted as usual and grinned at the technicians. They smiled back, their serrated teeth gleaming in the strange light of this new world. I clambered down and nodded the nod of success. There was much waving of tails but I didn't stop, not even when I passed the window, that strange invention we had borrowed from the extinct humans. Normally I would stop and look out on the beautiful world we Dromon had made but tonight I was too tired.

At my burrow I paused, conscious of a strange lethargy and a shimmering in the air. Fatigue sang in my bones like wind among the rocks. I pushed inside and fell onto the bed. Something hard lay under an arm. I shifted my claw and looked down. A strap, two in fact, one on each side. Conscious of a strange perversion, as though soiling myself, still I could not help it. I lay back and closed the lock.

End

EPITAPH
by Matt Jones

My breath catches in my throat,
Fingers slowly trembling,
And muscles as numb as a fish on land.
I hear her whistling down my ears
Though I cannot see her.
I can still feel her silky hair

Life is precious but can sometimes be treated as dispos-
  -able
I cannot retake what was once mine
Love is consuming
It claws at me from the chest
My belly groans with pain.

Through the mirror I see my shattering face,
I realised that I must subside my fear,
Rejoice for what has been given
And not what is lost.
I would run towards something and not away.

Throughout time I gained strength,
I gained faith,
I climbed up the mountain
And placed down the flag
Where I found self-confidence and inner tranquillity.

I remember the good, the bad,
The life that I cherished
Had made me who I am today.
I finally let go
And could see my face in the mirror again
As clear as day and bright as ever.

I thank you, instead of mourn.
She taught me that emotions remind us how to enjoy
 life
Even under the storm.
I found myself and could walk without fumbling
Look at my friends the same way as I did,
Eat without deteriorating,
And cry with tears of joy.

End

A FAIRY-TALE ENDING
By Mark Horne

We all know the stories. What happened next?

1. The giant fell from the beanstalk, his oversized clogs embedding themselves in the ground in a nearby country estate, creating two new homes for indentured servants who had hitherto been sleeping with the animals in the barns. The giant's enormous bones weren't prone to breaking from moderate heights, so he survived the drop, though he did have a sore scalp for several days, and had to sew some new slippers using several sacks used for carrying barley to market. It took three years for a new beanstalk to grow tall enough for him to reach his home among the clouds.

2. Goldilocks had always hated her nickname. She was called Elizabeth, for goodness' sake. It was just silly. They didn't call Susan "Rediplaits", and they didn't call Rachel "Mouseybrowncurls". They did call Ewan "Baldy", but kids can be so cruel. Goldilocks, who was called Elizabeth, never did tell anyone about her adventures in the woods. Who'd believe that bears would prepare porridge? Everyone knows that bears are carnivores. Later, during her studies for her Zoology degree, she learned that Eurasian Brown Bears are actually omnivores, but by then it was surely far too late to tell such a silly story.

3. Hansel still woke with a start every night, the image of a burning old woman peeling and charring and disintegrating in a flaming oven fresh in his mind's eye.

The witch's treasure had proven a curse for his father, who acquired a taste for peach schnapps and drank himself into an early grave. Gretel had seen her father's demise coming and wisely invested her share of the jewels in the sort of education that a poor woodcutter's daughter could never normally have afforded. She became a successful confectionery merchant in the city by the sea, and always ensured any leftover stock was sent to the local poor house for the children. Hansel meanwhile lived out his days in a very well-appointed mansion on the edge of the woods, never marrying, always awaking in a pool of his own sweat and fearing the moment that the crone's charred corpse would find its way back to him, to finish the meal she had started preparing all those years before.

4. The princess married the simpering prince, though she did insist that the prince's mother - who carried years of internalised misogyny and superstitions, acquired by growing up in a patriarchal society which placed enormous emphasis on dynastic marriage and created unnecessary problems through strict enforcement of primogeniture - seek professional counselling, lest she start placing peas under their planned children's beds in a fit of paranoia. Despite being something of an arranged marriage, and a blind one at that, she usually got on well with her husband, although she did draw the line at his plan to place the infamous pea in a museum. Some things are private.

End

LUPUS
by Matt Jones

Caw, caw, mortem has stalked him since I grew,
I crawled through him like a cockroach
he craved an appetite for freedom.
The wind whispers to him a sound when he reproaches,
Caw…

He was at the brink of innovation
as the current flailed his legs shattering the mirror.
Bleed with crimson was temptation
as was bitterness that was drawing nearer.
Caw…

No longer did he feel the constraint
he was turning rash.
He had swayed away starving
feasting on the fear within.
Caw…

Where light shines
he hisses away in the shadow,
he bays down as the predator he is.
His ears wail,
Caw…

As he tilted his head to Selene
I heard his sough through the free air.
The bark decayed and the leaves strewn

everything in the past was just a blur,
Caw…

We are no longer grey
for I made him my prey.
He danced in the clan
and snarls at the face of man
Caw…

Still at night I see mortem stalk me
always roosting on top of a branch with a quelling look
and forever more it will always say,
Caw…

End

Authors Note: -

- The poem symbolises a man who has social anxiety and feels more connected with nature. He loves wolves and thinks that he is one inside, so that narrative is described in third person with another identity (the wolf in him) narrating his change of character.

- Mortem represents a raven who follows the narrator like most raven that would often follow wolves to scavenge as much as a third of what wolves kill.

- Bay is the way a wolf sits.

- The spirit of wolf comes down as a list of;

- Sharp intelligence, deep connection with instincts

- Appetite for freedom

- Expression of strong instincts

- Feeling threatened, lack of trust in someone or in yourself

- I have called the title Lupus because lupus is Latin for wolf and it is also associated with a long-term condition that causes joint pain, skin rashes and tiredness. One of the symptoms is the sensitivity to light, where the light represents the bright city landscape and people that walk amongst the woods.

- 'We are no longer grey' – the man and the wolf portray each other like Yin and Yang, being the light and the shadow that bring a balance to the world. So, that means that the Yin and Yang has broken apart, making him feel more connected to the wolves than he does with humanity.

THE PSYCHO PE*IS PRUNER AT NUMBER 2
by Rowland Cook

You didn't need to be a doctor to tell that Jim wasn't well. Shambling along in a faded jacket, jeans and sneakers muttering to himself, most people avoided him. I didn't have the heart so I spoke to him; well, I spoke *at* him, civilly. The trouble was, the jumbled stream of speech that flowed from him was impossible to follow.

He ran a hand through his bushy shock of white hair, "Spock went to school with my mother," he informed me. I smiled at him. Chortling like a child with a funny secret he carried on, "Benito Mussolini saw grandfather time tells prisoners aren't right, you'll see."

"Really?" I replied (what on earth *do* you say to something like that?) The chortling went on,

"The Government's in on it, divorced fathers suffer in the space time continuum!" he said, nodding to underline the importance of this latest top-secret information.

He was sitting at the table next to mine now, confident of a willing audience. He was giggling and rocking backwards and forwards. I sighed inside, sometimes he babbled a couple of things and then ambled off. But I was in for the whole coffee long experience this time. *Wonderful!*

"Nice weather today." I ventured hoping without hope for a sensible response.

"Don't use the can of meat!" He was suddenly still, eyes wide open. It was like the voice came from inside my head. "Symptoms: - death within 24 hours, 80% fatality rate."

I blinked and went to ask him where that came from, but he was instantly back to his usual giggling, rocking self. "Have you seen Downton Abbey is not able to walk far in high heels?" and so it went on. I nodded and responded as best I could.

Back home, I decided to make myself a lazy bolognese. Put one can of stewing steak into a pan and add a can of chopped tomatoes. Throw in a tablespoon of tomato puree and add a generous tablespoon of Italian Herbs. Finally administer a sprinkle of garlic granules, and season to taste. Hey presto! instant bolognese.

The can of stewing steak was right at the back of the cupboard. Its lid was slightly domed and when the can opener bit down, gravy sprayed out and peppered my shirt. Dabbing at the offending brown spots at the sink, cursing, Jim's wide eyed message replayed in my brain.

"Don't use the can of meat......."

I tried to ignore the clammy wet patches sticking to my chest and sniffed at the can. It smelt OK. I shrugged; silly, nonsense, Jim. The can hovered over the saucepan as I dithered. There was something un-nerving about the way that warning had landed. I stood there, telling myself not to be silly, steam rising from the bubbling spaghetti. Then I wimped out and tipped the can into Fido's bowl. I had some proper mince in the fridge that needed eating up anyway. Dilemma solved!

I put the bowl outside for Fido but the big dog from number twelve ran up, and snatched the whole bowl the moment my back was turned. Fido's only little, he didn't even get a bite. That *bloody* dog! It was the bane of my life. I was furious, someone had to do something about it.

#

Two days later, the RSPCA turned up at the door in the form of a uniformed blond who didn't look too happy.

"Are you Samantha Elkington?" she asked rather too brusquely for my liking.

145

I nodded, "What do you want?" I retorted, irritated at the interruption.

"Is this your bowl?" she asked, the officiousness in her voice big, square and made of bricks.

I didn't like her tone. "How should I know?" I responded, trying to match her, "There are thousands of bowls just like that in shops up and down the country."

Blondie bad-mood turned the bowl over, "This one has your name and address engraved on the bottom."

Oh Bollocks!!!........ busted! I felt my face go red and hated myself for it. That bloody dog from number 12. Right! Time for plan 'B' which I had been working on since the bowl snatching incident. "Come in," I said as sweetly as possible between gritted teeth, "I have something you should see."

I had been trawling my CCTV footage from the burglar alarm system. "Here's that blasted dog digging up £400 of bedding plants whilst I was out.... now here it is crapping all over my lawn... having a piss on the wheel of my car ..... chasing my dog to the point of trauma. Finally, stealing that bowl after I put a can of stewing steak out for Fido. What are you going to do about that?"

Fido brushed up against her legs wagging his tail. Blondie bad-mood looked down at the irresistible little cockapoo and seemed to soften a little around the edges. "You'd better take a look in my van," she replied, "*I* have something *you* should see."

A dog was laid out in the back of the van, cold, milky-eyed and stone dead. I recognised the 'bad dog from number twelve' as I'd christened it. "It looks like the food in your bowl was the cause." she said, "The owner alleges you deliberately poisoned it. Do you still have the can?"

I opened the lid of the grey wheelie bin. "Got any gloves??"

That can had far reaching consequences. The local shop was closed for a week and its entire stock of canned goods confiscated. Bought from an Eastern European supplier of dubious scruples apparently. A lot of re-working of sell by dates going on, allegedly. People were contacted all over the locality and a can recall request featured on the news.

Luckily, no one else got ill. It was botulinus, some sort of secreted toxin—all very complicated. I looked it up on the computer at home. Guess what! - the symptoms were listed as 'death within 24 hours, 80% fatality rate.' All the hairs on the back of my neck stood on end. How the hell had Jim known?

The shop didn't survive and I quickly got tired of people being sad that it had closed. It was like it was all my fault?!

The scene I had with the ex dog-owning tattooed gobshite from number twelve ended badly too. I was out in the front garden with my weedkiller spray in one hand and the secateurs in the other, when he came marching by with his partner in tow.

"You *fucking* killed my dog." he yelled, full of rage.

His partner tried to calm him down, "No Bill, it was an accident."

He turned and slapped her, hard.

"Don't …" was as far as he got.

All I remember is a red mist for the next few minutes, but in court, his partner said I went berserk. It seems I sprayed him in the face with weedkiller and delivered a kick to his danglers that sent him sprawling. A witness said she pulled me off him as I went for his nose with the secateurs screaming I'd prune his wotsit off if he ever hit her again.

Well,……. you know,………. I was upset with him.

I walked out of court with an ASBO, I mean, *me!!!* I wasn't allowed within 100 yards of them. That was tricky, they only lived 60 yards up the road. Unfortunately, a couple of days later a brick came crashing through the front room window. Fortunately, the tattooed gobshite was caught on my CCTV and disappeared into thin air, probably too embarrassed to stay around. She took her black eye home to mum, I got a bunch of flowers and a card saying 'Thanks for sticking up for me'. That was nice.

The local paper ran it as a story and overnight I was unofficially dubbed the 'psycho pe*is pruner at number 2'. Life suddenly got very trying. People looking, pointing, children sniggering. I was even asked for my autograph a couple of times. I got paranoid about even looking at a pair of secateurs and stayed in a lot. Eventually, after several weeks, the fuss died down and life got back to a state I call 'almost normal'.

It was my first time back in the coffee shop, when who should come along but Jim.

"The train to Mars is running backwards today, Ebenezer Scrooge's President's biscuit tin's covered in fish scales," he giggled.

"Jim, you saved my life with that comment about the can." I said.

It was true. But for him, I'd have eaten my lazy bolognese and died. It said on the internet that botulinus isn't destroyed by cooking. It had really made me reflect on how life and death are sometimes separated by the tiniest random happenings.

He looked at me wide eyed and still, "You're welcome. Go buy a lottery ticket." The voice in my head sounded very sure of itself. Jim ambled off and I put down my coffee and headed straight for WHS. Maybe my finances were about to pick up?

One thing was for certain, I'd be much more generous about talking to Jim from now on.

End

BANQUO'S GHOSTS
by Martin Hilyard

I'm writing this account because I am the last original member of the crew. I emphasise the word 'original' for reasons you'll understand later. If you're reading this you will by now have encountered the strange creatures I mockingly, but not without a little pride, nicknamed Banquo's Ghosts. Kelvin always called them, unfairly, clockworks They weren't, as he found out to his cost when they killed him.

But to get back to the point. Of the nine members of the Deep Space Vessel "Thane of Cawdor" only I, Alasdair Banquo, survive. Or if you're reading this, don't survive. None of the strange, more than real creatures perhaps pouring you coffee or telling you about growing up in Connecticut or Warsaw, none of them are real and all of them killed us.

Let every man be master of his time....

That's right, killed us. Oh, some of us committed suicide, like Horowitz. I won't deny it. How could I? You'll see it all for yourselves. They're such hams and love to replay just how they, or I should say we, died. But perhaps I'm getting ahead of myself. I ought to tell you our story before they tell you themselves. That way you'll know the truth, whatever that is.

As I said, this is the "Thane of Cawdor," a scientific expedition to investigate the deep space anomaly that we now know to be the first real Black Hole. We were thrilled of course. But the excitement really got going when we detected the cluster of spaceships orbiting the anomaly, just short of the event horizon. We programmed for orbit, not contact, which was just as well for hyperatomic engines don't work near a Black Hole. But then, if you're watching this, you know that. You've been trapped like us and all the others before us. Or maybe not. Maybe you don't use hyperatomic engines. Maybe you thought yourself here and can think yourself back. If so, congratulations. If not, welcome to the show.

At first we focussed all our energies on trying to escape. But then we started to notice things weren't right. Campbell and Lusardi said they would go to the engine room to see if they could get the hyperdrive working. They never came back. After a couple of days someone went after them and came back, pale and - I hate to say it - haunted. The two men had died of old age trying to walk there. We found their dessicated corpses about a hundred meters along when we swung into orbit and the effects subsided. Their ancient, wizened faces hit us hard, like a life of dedication betrayed.

Come, night, scarf up the tender eye of pitiful day.....

Time gets warped along the dorsal axis, we discovered. Crossing from one side of the ship to the other was like moving from the future through the present and into a pitiable past. We'd encounter ourselves, shadows and ghosts. An endless fool's parade of miserable, defeated old men from the future and simpletons from the past, all of whom were us. As they multiplied they seemed to become more real. Saying things we never said, doing things we never did, either in the past or later. Then we realised we had clockworks of our own.

So there we were, safe in orbit but stuck for good. No-one could rescue us because all our ships use hyperatomic engines. (I won't tell you what planet we're from, you might be 12 feet high with warlike intent). And us with the biggest archaeological find of all, spaceships maybe millions of years old. Imagine our surprise when we discovered there were also creatures on board, real live aliens. And our shock when we discovered they weren't real, they were clockworks as well. Or as I call them, Banquo's Ghosts.

At first it was like being Robinson Crusoe. Sure we were stranded in this strange island in space but it was filled with wonders. Aliens, or at least their ghosts. Different to us in every way conceivable yet all willing to talk. And boy, how they liked to talk (or think or shake their tentacles at us like some insane mime show). Yet over time our interest waned. One by one the others drifted away, back to the ship.

I asked Kelvin about that and he looked at me like I was something that had crawled out from under a rock. Aalpeter explained it, maybe; he said it made him feel dirty. In a couple of the ships, though, the Ghosts were humanoid and in one they didn't use language but telepathy. I could talk to them. I'd just think at them and sometimes they'd think back, telling some tale or saying something using semantic symbols even my poor brain could understand. And with their thoughts came alien smells and sounds, experiences hinted at like senile memories, but sweet, sad. They didn't really talk back. We never held a conversation, they were still living the lives of the original crew. It was frustrating, believe me. I'd be telling them my life story when they'd get up and walk off, begin trying to repair their engines or cook a non-existent meal or go to their sleeping quarters and fuck, if you could call what they did fucking.

After a few months, things started falling apart. We spent more and more time with the Ghosts, even though we knew what was likely to happen. As long as we were alive they could not really live themselves, could never be us. I don't know what happened to Kelloway. She died in the biolab with no-one to bind her wounds. Horowitz committed suicide soon after that. Aalpeter disappeared. I never did find out what happened to him. I suppose he fell down somewhere, blind drunk, and didn't get up. Or maybe decided to push the wrong button somewhere, like an airlock or crammed into a waste disposal chute, and blammo!

I suppose I should take some blame for that. I did something the others couldn't cope with. I fell in love with a Ghost. There was one, a female from out Altair way. Her people were humanoid to the nth degree, as much as we could tell. Seeing Kelvin's Ghost merge with him gave me an idea. Perhaps I could do it with her.

She was dating this other one, a tall, handsome buck. They'd make love. Often. Maybe it was their way of coping with despair. I used to watch them. I'd sit in a chair in their cabin while they had sex, occasionally reading a book as I watched or sipping a cup of coffee. They didn't seem to mind. But that pissed off the others, just by itself. They started avoiding me, even their Ghosts. Then I did something worse. As I said, I fell in love, which in that place and time was the stupidest thing a man could do. But I couldn't help it, and truth to tell I never thought I would. She was everything to me. I thought I'd be happy the rest of my life. Boy, was I wrong.

One day I went to her cabin and found them together, her and her alien lover. They were Ghosts, they had no real emotions, no memories. They were clockworks, aping us or themselves or I don't know what. I pulled out a pistol and shot him, shot them both. But it made no difference. The next day there she was, making eggs and asking me what I'd like to do at the weekend.

I stopped spending so much time with the Ghosts then, apologised to the rest of the crew and tried to find my way

153

back to the real world. It didn't last. Listening to Aalpeter and Kiefer and the rest grumbling, futilely discussing the situation, bored me. They sank into their own private world of fear and bitterness and hate.

Tomorrow, and tomorrow, and tomorrow.....

Our orbit was slowly deteriorating, month by month and time was starting to stretch. You can only squeeze so much hope out of the oily rag of a clockwork's false - no, fake - emotions. In the end I jetted over to one of the alien ships, intent on living my own life in the time I had left but found no-one was interested. The Ghosts were mainly following other Ghosts and none of them had time for me.

Then I noticed something. Things had changed. I found some of the Ghosts working on the engines, changing things. They looked weird. And then I saw what it was. They were amalgams, the Ghosts of the other aliens had merged with them, imperfectly. Bits hung out here and there. As I watched the images settled down, cleared and they were as I remember them, my dear dead friends.

Could they get the engines working after all? I tasted something sweet for a moment, only to find bitter dregs at the bottom of my cup. I saw me killed. I hadn't realised just how much real life interfered with their existence and how - despite the fact that all of us had been selected for our stable temperaments and rationality - they could learn to hate. They were us after all.

It was my alien lover who did it. Or her ghost. I never did find out. Perhaps the ghost of a ghost. She may not have been real, but boy could she kill. After that, being in love with her didn't seem quite so attractive.

Anyway, I'm dead, though if you bump into me somewhere, why not buy me a cup of coffee, as we used to say. I'm a bit of a bookworm but still good company. That's all I can tell you. You'll work out the rest by just talking to us. Or perhaps not. Goodbye, until I see you again.

Beneath her feet came the steady purr of the engines. She pressed the erase button and turned back to the book she had been avidly reading.

Life's but a walking shadow....

End

A TINY WILD WOOD SONGBIRD
by Joy S. Buchanan

A tiny wild wood songbird sat
Atop a grey green lime tree
He sang all through the winter night
His voice was loudly ringing.

Oh, sing to me, oh sing to me
You tiny wild wood songbird
I'll bind your feathers all around
With gold and silk and satin.

Oh, keep your gold, oh keep your silk
I'll sing now for another
I am a wild wood songbird free
And there's no man shall own me.

Fly up into the valley cold
The frost will freeze your body
The frost may freeze, the frost so cold
My love the sun will warm me.

End

GOOD WILL
by Mark Horne

I want to tell you a story about Christmas. Heart-warming, touching, bittersweet. All of that festive cliché.

For the first time in years I'm in the pub on Christmas Eve.

The kid is a teenager now, the rituals of new pyjamas and milk for Santa now too childish, and she's out with friends, perhaps at the pictures, or perhaps in with friends and sneaking eggnog or fruit cider at some lucky parent's house while they're also out. Either way, it leaves Mum and Dad to go out drinking by ourselves, both of us excited at the unusual opportunity and equally aware of the early bereft hint of a future empty nest.

We go to the Bells on the main road, a lot nicer than it used to be, according to a friend who worked here in her teenage years and used to tell tales that are now brushed under the carpet of adult respectability and parenthood, as if they never took place.

But little reminder of the pub's past still lingers on this cold, wet Yuletide night in Liverpool, even among the music, merriness and good-natured laughter.

Kevin is away at the bar getting a round in and Louise and the wife are in the Ladies' room. The door opens and a woman dashes in, shouting a man's name. She glances about and I see she's wearing cotton pyjama pants that are sodden and grey at the bottom under her parka, before she dashes up to the bar and doesn't stop until she gets the

157

landlord's attention. Whatever it is she wants, he doesn't seem about to give it to her.

And in that moment, I recall my own past. A summer job in a small off-licence, straight out of school. A drawn, tired, middle-aged woman who lived in the flat above the shop and who would venture down every day or so in her dressing gown to buy a bottle of cheap white rum.

One day she came in when I was alone on shift, wearing the usual garb of dirty greying-pink pyjama bottoms. Could I sub her for a bottle? No, I'd said, I could not. She didn't argue.

I felt bad though. I mean, I wasn't a good store-keeper. The offie was alone, between two empty units in a small bank of shops, and thanks to a couple of the older scally kids we had a problem with loss prevention that I hadn't exactly taken heroic actions to stem. But I couldn't very well hand this woman a bottle from behind the counter now, could I?

I'd mentioned this incident to my boss, a man only a few years my senior, the next time he was in. Thought nothing of it.

A week later, at shift changeover, the boss told me what he'd done. He laughed as he recounted the story. Our pyjama-clad upstairs neighbour had come in during the week and he'd mentioned, falsely, that men were looking for her. Bailiffs, possibly. He'd laughed again, proud of himself. She'd upped and left her flat that very day.

I smiled weakly, not wanting to contradict my boss, but aware that there was something sickening in his pleasure at his actions. She did no harm. She had a boy. We sold her the drug that fed her habit, for fuck's sake.

And now I look at the woman at the bar who reminds me of my past shame.

I want to go to her, buy her a Christmas drink, find out who this man is, who she's lost, and make sure she gets home safe, on this night of all nights.

I want to tell you that uplifting Christmas story of goodwill to all. But as I'm about to rise, Kev is back with a round. The girls are back from the lav. Toasts are made, jokes are attempted, drinks are supped, and when I next look to the bar, she's gone.

End

THE COACH HOUSE
by Victoria Stewart

They were looking forward to having Christmas in their new place. On the first Saturday in December, Mark suggested to Anna that they should go across the Common and into the woods to see if they could find some holly, or even mistletoe, to decorate the house. They wrapped up because it was frosty, and wondered what to wear on their feet, because they still hadn't got any proper shoes for walking in the countryside.

The ground was frozen hard, making it heavy going. They tramped with their heads down, holding hands, his in a leather glove, hers in a woolly mitten. When a few birds of some sort suddenly flew up out of the undergrowth, Mark felt Anna grip his fingers as she gave a nervous laugh.

"It's strange to think there used to be a house here," she said, knocking the heel of her boot against a tussock. "Maybe if we dig down, we'll find some cool Victorian floor tiles we can salvage."

"We've got cool floor tiles already, we don't need to salvage any," said Mark.

They were almost at the woods now and he glanced back in the direction they'd come from. The sun was low and bright, and, just for a moment, a dark shape swam across his field of vision. He narrowed his eyes: it was almost as though the old house had suddenly reared up again. He blinked the shadow away, turned, took a step, and went over on his ankle, stumbling.

"You OK?" said Anna.

"Yeah."

He inspected his shoe, which was crusted with frozen mud. Then he noticed something else underfoot. He bent and picked it up.

"What is it?" said Anna.

"Dunno – thought it was a brooch, or something but – dunno."

He showed her. It was a piece of metal work, rusted and dirty, a piece of—who could tell what? A grid about three or four inches square made of delicate barley sugar twists, with a point like an arrow at one corner, a curve like the finial on their bedroom curtain pole at another, small rosettes in the form of flowers where the bars crossed.

"Is it a pot-stand or something?" said Anna.

"You could use it for that. Must be from the old house. Maybe there *are* tiles under there."

He gestured towards the frosted ground. They'd moved in among the trees now, and the other side of the Common seemed further away, a long walk back. It was colder in the wood than it was in the open; he'd thought it would be the other way around.

"Just leave it," said Anna. "It's dirty."

She was right. It had sharp edges and after he dropped it, he had to brush his hands together to get the crumbs of rust and soil off his gloves.

They didn't have any secateurs, but he'd brought the sharp scissors from the kitchen and when they found a holly bush, not far into the woods, he fished them out of the back pocket of his jeans. The bush had lots of berries and looked quite Christmassy, but the stems were thicker than he'd expected, and he had to open up the scissors and use the blade like a saw. He snagged his scarf and got hot, and Anna wasn't much help because she didn't want to mess up her coat, but eventually they had what looked like

161

plenty and he put it in the big carrier bag he'd picked up as they left the house.

"I hope we're not breaking some bye-law," Anna said.

"I never thought of that. Can't do any harm, surely."

He looked around. He could see now that what they'd been calling 'the wood' was quite a small clump of trees, really.

"Shall we just see what's out the other side?" he said, and Anna looked to where they'd come from, then looked in the opposite direction, and then looked at him and gave a shrug.

They walked on a bit further, and when they emerged, they were confronted by what seemed to be an impassable mass of low, spiky bushes. Beyond the bushes, maybe a few hundred yards away, stood a pair of gateposts. They were square, a couple of feet across and twelve or more tall, and they had carved stone figures on top of them. On the right, Mark thought he could see the antlers of a deer, or a stag, rather, and on the left, well, it was hard to tell, but perhaps that was the mane of a lion.

"Must be all that's left of the house," said Anna.

"I suppose so," said Mark.

Anna had got her phone out, and, slipping one of her mittens off, she took a picture, and then pinched it into close-up with her fingers.

"We're on the wrong side, aren't we?" said Mark. 'You need to be coming in from over there to see them properly.'

It was strange, he thought, that he'd never noticed them when he'd been driving along the main road out of the village, which was surely over in the distance, though he couldn't hear any traffic.

"Hmm," said Anna.

She showed him her phone. In her photograph, the grey stone of the gate-posts looked black, and the shapes of the creatures were silhouetted against the sky, which was such a pale blue that it seemed almost white. Mark was about to ask her if he could have a closer look when she swiped the picture away and put her phone in her pocket. She pulled her mitten on and gave a shudder.

"Getting cold now," she said. "Let's go."

By the time they were on the Common again, the sun had almost disappeared and there were pink strips of cloud across the sky.

"Lovely," said Anna, holding onto his arm, turning her face upwards, then burying it in her scarf. "Really cold, though," she said, and he put his arm around her shoulder and pulled her towards him, gave her a squeeze, and then released her, took her hand, and picked up his pace. He wanted to get home; it was starting to get dark, and she was right, it was getting colder.

Things had been better between them since they'd moved. The travelling had been getting him down, getting them both down, and the compromise seemed to be working out. Anna had managed to arrange her teaching at the university so that she could get the train first thing on Monday, stay a couple of nights with her friend Claire, and usually be home in time for dinner on Wednesday. He had a thirty-minute drive to the Institute, rather than the best-part-of-two-hours slog each way that had confronted him when they lived in London. And they'd managed to swap their tiny flat for a house, an old coach house, in fact, with stripped floors, original beams, a refitted kitchen and enough rooms for Anna to have a study, and for there to be a spare bedroom, though they hadn't really felt like having people to stay just yet, not while they were settling in.

The village had most of what you'd need, a decent Indian, couple of pubs, miniature Sainsbury's, and the butcher where Mark had ordered a goose for Christmas dinner. There were footpaths along the river, and the Common was just at the end of their road. It seemed strange that no one had ever reused that land, the Common, and when they'd had their viewing, they'd been concerned about it; they didn't want to end up next door to a building site. But the solicitor had told them there was a covenant of some kind protecting it from development.

On the way back that afternoon, Mark looked at the information board that had been erected near the dog waste bin by the Parish Council, but there was nothing about the gate-posts. At the top it said, 'Former site of Norries Hall' and there were drawings of the wildlife you might see. Those birds might have been pheasants. In the bottom right-hand corner, there was a short paragraph that said that Norries Hall had been built in the 1870s for the Norries family and that it'd been destroyed in a fire in 1925. There was a black and white photograph of a house, but it had got quite weathered and you couldn't really make out what the place had been like, except that it had tall windows, and that there were pillars on either side of the front door.

"Burned down," said Mark, pointing to the picture.

"Or 'went on fire'," Anna said, making quotation marks with her fingers. "Maybe they changed their minds and it was an insurance job."

Mark had been wondering whether anyone had died in the fire, and thought that what Anna had said was bit heartless, but it wasn't worth getting into an argument about, so he just said, "Glad our coach house survived at least."

When they got home, they tipped the holly out of the bag onto the floor of the porch and left it there overnight so that any insect life could make its getaway. The next afternoon, Mark put his gloves on again to bring two big handfuls into the sitting room while Anna cleared some of the pictures and other oddments off the mantelpiece. They already had a few Christmas cards, and she put those to one side while they carefully arranged the boughs of leaves and berries. Then, before they'd quite finished, something clanked onto the tiles on the hearth.

"What's that?" Anna said.

They both looked. Anna crouched, and with her finger and thumb picked something out of the remnants that had dropped down there.

"Why did you bring this back?" she said.

It was the piece of metalwork that he'd picked up yesterday.

"I didn't. I left it there, you saw me," he said.

"That's weird." They looked at it.

"It must have got caught up in the holly somehow."

He knew it sounded unconvincing but didn't know what else to say. There didn't seem to be an explanation.

"Do you want to go and chuck it outside?" she said, offering it to him, and he took it in his still-gloved fingers. He didn't ask why she didn't just take it outside herself. He went to the back door and was about to skim it down the garden, but then hesitated. He examined it: it was dirty and damaged, but someone had spent time on it, making it, you could see that even if you didn't know anything about that sort of thing. Instead of just chucking it, he stepped outside and slotted it down behind the little wooden shelter up against the wall, where the logs were kept. There was just enough space for it in the narrow gap.

They agreed that it was one of the nicest Christmases they'd had, much nicer to be out here in the countryside than in London. The goose was a bit greasy but it was nice to have a change from turkey. They even went to the Carol Service in the village church and joked with each other that they were becoming old fogies, but it suited them, how their life was now. Eventually, though, it was time for the decorations to come down.

Anna was tidying away the cards and gathering up the holly when she said, "Oh God, what's this?"

Mark was taking the Christmas tree out into the garden, and when he heard her, he dumped it by the kitchen door and went back in.

"What's the matter?"

She gestured towards the mantelpiece.

"Look at it."

He went and looked. The pale wood, which before Christmas had been smooth and clean, protected with a layer of matt varnish, was now marked with scratches, deeper surely than holly leaves could make.

He saw that Anna was upset and said, "Don't worry. It won't be hard to fix. I can go and get the stuff later, if you want."

"What's done it though?"

He ran his fingers over the marred surface, then pulled his hand away, not wanting to get splinters. He shrugged and shook his head, trying to think what he could say to make things better, but she suddenly bent down and picked something up from the rug.

"I thought you threw this away?" she said.

She was holding the piece of metalwork, the one they'd found that day in the woods.

"I did," he said, confused. "Don't you remember? We brought it back by accident, and I took it outside. I shoved it down the back of the wood store."

He couldn't read her expression; did she think he was playing some sort of practical joke on her?

"Down the back of the wood store?"

"Yeah."

"Why didn't you put it in the bin?"

"I don't know, I know it's broken and messy but it seemed a shame to just throw it away. But I will, I'll just put it in the bin."

He took it from her again, and went outside, and opened the bin and dropped it in on top of the bin bags. Then, confused, he went and slipped the ends of his fingers into the space where he thought he'd left it between the wood store and the wall. As far as he could tell, there was nothing there. Well, of course, there wouldn't be, would there?

Anna seemed a bit subdued that evening, but when he asked her if there was anything wrong, she just said, "You know, Sunday feeling." Although term didn't start for another week, she had to go to London for meetings in the morning. They went to bed quite early, and after he'd put the light off, she surprised him by turning towards him and reaching for him, and they found each other gently in the dark.

The next night, when Anna was at Claire's, something unpleasant happened. She'd phoned at about nine, when Mark was flicking desultorily between channels, already thinking about turning in, and they'd had the usual 'how was your day' conversation.

"It's gloomy here without the decorations up," he said.

"Aw, missing the decorations? Rather hoped you might be missing me."

"Missing you, too. Thinking about last night, that was nice."

"It *was* nice." He could hear her breathing. "Well, don't think about it too hard. I should be home before you tomorrow."

He was going to ask her if the train had been busy, but then he heard a voice in the background and Anna laughing and saying something back that he couldn't make out. It was probably Claire he could hear. He'd never met her, and in fact Anna had never really mentioned her until she'd told him that Claire had offered to have her to stay. She was a couple of years older than Anna and came from Northern Ireland, and her flat was on the other side of London from where they'd lived. That was about all he knew about her.

"Sorry," said Anna, "I'd better go, few things to finish."

He went to bed not long after they'd hung up and lay there for a while listening to music, thinking that he should stop off and buy some flowers for her on the way home from work, to make up for the house looking so empty without the holly and the tree, but soon he found that he wasn't thinking about Anna, or at least not about seeing her the next day, and not about what had happened between them the night before either. He was thinking about what she'd said that day on the Common, about digging down and finding old floor tiles, and then about the joke she'd made when they were first looking round the house with the estate agent, you shall go to the ball, how they'd have to be home by midnight, because the guy had told them about it having been built as a coach house, and at some point he must have fallen asleep because when he woke up the lamp and the radio were both off, and he was lying flat on his back and a breathy voice seemed to be emanating from the corner of the dark room, missing me, missing me, and he thought, has she come secretly from London to surprise me, but when he tried to sit up, tried to speak, he found that there was a tremendous weight holding him down against the mattress, hands on his shoulders pressing tight against his bones, someone's chest on his chest, so heavy that he could barely breathe, let alone utter a word, but he could hear breaths rasping in his ear now, no words, then a sound like the sound of metal on stone, and for what seemed like minutes but was perhaps only a second he felt helpless: speechless; paralysed.

When he came to himself, he was lying curled up on his side, his heart racing. It was still dark, and he couldn't tell what time it was. He flicked on the lamp and saw that it was just before seven, time to get up, but he felt exhausted, as though he hadn't slept at all. He'd heard of this, what had just happened to him: sleep paralysis it was called. He put the radio on, wanting some noise to ground him in the real world. It was a physiological phenomenon, that was all, no matter how real it had felt. He lay there trying to slow his breathing, but the sound of it disturbed him, and he pushed the duvet away and decided to go and make some coffee.

The first thing he saw when he put the kitchen light on was that piece of metal sitting there on the work surface. He felt sick, dizzy, couldn't bring himself to go into the kitchen at first. Then he thought, of course, if Anna was convinced that he'd deliberately brought it into the house before Christmas, as a joke of some sort, this might be her getting one up on him. But no, he was getting confused, it hadn't been here last night, and Anna was in London, he'd only imagined hearing her upstairs, she hadn't really come back.

He thought about taking a picture of it with his phone and sending it to her, asking her what the fuck, but he didn't know how she'd take it. He remembered how upset she'd been about the scratches on the mantelpiece, and then how quiet she'd been on Sunday night, how gentle, and he didn't want to upset her. Without really thinking about it, he went upstairs and pulled on some clothes. He took the metal ornament, or fragment, or whatever it was in his gloved hand and went out into the half-light of the cold morning and down the lane and onto Norries Common, then stumbled across and into the dark wood. He almost fell more than once as he scrambled through to the other side, where the low bushes seemed to ripple, like restless, spiny creatures arching their backs. He weighed the piece of metal in his hand, then holding it by a corner, he threw it and watched it spin out of sight, hearing, so he thought, a small noise as, somewhere towards the gateposts, it landed.

End

WINTER'S DUSK, SPRINGS DAWN
by Matthew Jones

My locks are being tugged
My skin is cold and cracked
My feet are so numb
That I could barely move.

I am blanketed with white
Which then turns to slush piles
when it is coming down on me,
my warmth is now in their grasp.

My pride has been ripped.
My brass coil is twisted and rotting
I am no longer lambent
With autumn's ember.

As time passes, the sun rests on my skin.
My hair starts to blossom
As green as May,
I feel warmth from the curtain of light.

I may not be evergreen
but I still stand, true and noble.
when fall comes I do not
I spring when I can.

The sounds of hymns through the river of air
has hydrated and patched my soul.
We maybe ordinary,
but we can also become extraordinary.

We must look at the bright side
Time can be cruel
But with patience comes reward
Trust your journey ahead.

End

Author's Note:

I've always thought of life being like a tree, we stress through the bad times that we may lose our hair or get blown at by cold words. But if we are patient we will be rewarded and we will continue to grow into something amazing, love yourself for what you are and what you can be. Be optimistic and blossom like the trees do, there is always a bright path ahead of us.

MEET THE AUTHORS

Mark Horne:

Mark was born in Manchester and now lives in Liverpool, where he works in Higher Education. He has previously been published in various magazines and regional newspapers and is currently a regular contributor to The Sceptic magazine. He has been writing fiction since childhood, but has not dipped his toe into publishing any stories until now. He is the current group organiser of the Liverpool Laid Back Writers.

Peter Glazebrook:

Peter is an ex civil servant of the British Government and ardent beekeeper. During a career that has covered work as a bioscientist and SCUBA diving instructor he has gathered a wealth of information that feeds into his writing.

Peter has taken his writing seriously for the last couple of years and is horrified at the amount of hard work required. He has previously published in Horror magazine and the 1st Degree crime anthology.

Ian Cragg:

Ian has had a lifelong interest in creative writing. From having a poem published in a local newspaper at the age of nine, through writing and performing in rag shows at secondary school, to having two novels published on Amazon Kindle in recent years, he has maintained a passion for the written word.

Taking early retirement in 2015 has allowed Ian to broaden his scope, trying his hand at playwriting for stage and radio as well as his first loves: short stories, novels and poetry. His involvement with the Laid Back Writers group has undoubtedly helped him develop with the benefit of feedback from other aspiring writers.

Rowland Cook:

Rowland is a Nuclear Installations Inspector living in Formby, Liverpool who started writing fiction about five years ago. Now in partial retirement he spends his free time writing, playing the guitar, cooking and trying to keep up with the long list of things to do his wife organises for him. He has been passionate about Science Fiction since he was young and aims ultimately to get a Sci-Fi novel published. He is currently aiming at improving his writing style and is the event organiser for the group.

Joy Buchanan:

Joy has been writing poems in English since childhood and has also produced a number of poems in translation from German some of which are published in full or in part on the internet, (www.brindinpress.com). She has also written articles, song lyrics, edited and published a book of Christian poetry as well as an African story for children published in French, German and English. She was a member of the Open University Alumni Poets Society and contributed to their magazine. She continues to write and translate poetry alongside her other commitments.

Her professional career has included work as a teacher of English as a foreign language, EN/GE correspondent and translator in the field of orthopaedics and traumatology. She is currently on the editorial board of Medpoetry: Healing Words (fb).

Suzie Sinclair-Wood:

Suzie put down a pen in Local Government managing critical social, hospital and emergency services to pick up a pen and write for pleasure and fun. Whilst not taking herself too seriously, she enjoys the pretensions of 'une flaneuse' living in the City, writing about, drawing and photographing its people, places and spaces. Her poetry and prose are published in a number of local anthologies and she's currently editing her first novel.

Ian Young:

Ian is a retired civil servant (eyes roll back) whose 40+ years in public service (eyes roll even further back) serve as an excuse, not an explanation, for why he has never tried to be a writer before.

Ian writes historical fiction (eyes now rolled so far back, only the whites are visible). Go on, give it a try! It's better than it sounds (he hopes).

Martin Hilyard:

Martin is a writer of primarily historical fiction though his latest work, Twenty Six Days, which tells the story of a man's search for a sister he left behind in Poland in 1939, combines historical events with a contemporary linking narrative.

His writing is crisp, straight to the point, captures the readers imagination and holds on to it. He is primarily interested in history, war and conflict and has a meticulous attention to detail. He is personable, engaging, serious, a thinker and a listener, and likes to write quickly and fluently.

He enjoys engaging with people about the craft of writing and likes nothing better than conversation. So if you're ever in Liverpool stand him a pint on a Saturday afternoon.

Luke Dawson:

Luke has been an aspiring writer for a number of years. He started off his career studying Media Production at the University of Lincoln specialising in Film and Screenwriting. While on an exchange program with Minnesota State University, Moorhead, he found a calling to writing when participating in their annual 48-hour film festival. By a fluke, he was chosen to write the film and it received the award for best writing. He has since completed several feature length scripts as well as a TV pilot script and sold a short film script to a Norwegian production company which has since been produced.

Luke's preference of genre is fantasy and science fiction however he likes to delve into other genres as a challenge to myself. Since joining the Liverpool Laidback Writer's Group, he writes, '*I have been inspired to challenge myself further by drafting short stories and even a fantasy epic. I am always looking towards my next project and hope to see more of my work published in the near future.*'

E J Hamer:

E J Hamer is a sporadic writer, taking the long scenic road to creative success.

A big fan of travel, large flowering trees and colourful objects. Has a real dislike of soup spoons.

Matthew Jones:

Matthew is a receptionist at Merseyside Police, living in Allerton, Liverpool who has taken an interest in writing since 2014. He first started writing poetry in school and entered one of his poems for a competition based on war, which was published in an anthology. He has moved on to do fantasy stories during his time at University.

He spends his free time walking his dog and taking pictures of the park, as well as sketching and baking. He has loved Science Fiction and Fantasy since his dad introduced him to Star Wars and Doctor Who at an early age. This together with his passion for art has fuelled his desire to write a series of books. He is aiming to improve his social and writing skills and hope to learn from the writer's group, so he can create a world of his own, through writing.

Victoria Stewart:

Victoria Stewart lives near Liverpool. Formerly an academic, she now works in an office. She's had flash fiction published by Reflex, Ellipsis Zine, and Flash Flood, and in the Bath Flash Fiction Anthology.

Liam Physick:

Liam lives in Crosby, near Liverpool. He has a wide variety of interests, including history, sport and the natural world. He enjoys reading, surfing the Internet and following major sporting events both online and on television. He maintains a blog,

'theinconvenientblogger.blogspot.com',

where he uploads his stories. The blog also contains several articles on various other matters that reflect his diverse interests.